LOST IN AMERICA

LOST IN AMERICA

By Marilyn Sachs

A DEBORAH BRODIE BOOK

ROARING BROOK PRESS
NEW MILFORD, CONNECTICUT

Copyright © 2005 by Marilyn Sachs

A Deborah Brodie Book
Published by Roaring Brook Press
A Division of Holtzbrinck Publishing Holdings Limited Partnership
143 West Street
New Milford, Connecticut 06776

LIBRARY OF CONGRESS CATALOGING-IN-PUBLICATION DATA

Sachs, Marilyn.
 Lost in America / Marilyn Sachs.—1st ed.
 p. cm.
 "A Deborah Brodie book."
 Summary: Follows the experiences of Nicole, a teenaged French Jew,
 from 1943 to 1948, as she loses her parents and sister to the
 concentration camps and then leaves her native France to make a new life for herself
 in New York City.
 ISBN   1-59643-040-0
 [1. Immigrants—Fiction. 2. Jews—United States—Fiction. 3. New York
 (N.Y.)—History—1898–1951—Fiction. 4. Jews—France—Fiction. 5.
 Holocaust, Jewish (1939–1945)—France—Fiction. 6.
 France—History—German occupation, 1940–1945—Fiction.] I. Title.
 PZ7.S1187Lo 2005
 [Fic]--dc22
                                   2004017551

10 9 8 7 6 5 4 3 2 1

Book design by BTDNYC
Printed in the United States of America
First edition

To Fanny Krieger,
with the deepest affection and admiration

LOST IN AMERICA

CHAPTER 1

November 1943
Aix-les-Bains, France

I didn't kiss my parents on that last night in November.

MAMA HAD BEEN BUSY preparing dinner for our friends, the Restons, who were leaving our town the next morning for Switzerland. Mama had managed to find a chicken and some vegetables, and was hoping that there would be enough food for two families.

Many Jewish families had already fled, but my father refused to believe there was any real danger. He listened to the British Broadcasting Corporation broadcasts every night. The Germans, he told us, were retreating everywhere in Russia. The BBC reported that the Allies were advancing in Italy, and Mussolini had already been deposed.

"The war will be all over in a few months," he kept saying.

Mama argued with him, pointing out that so many Jews all over France had been taken away by the Gestapo—nobody knew where.

"But not here," my father insisted. "Why would they bother with a small town like this, especially now that they're losing the war?"

That last night was a happy one. Mama spoke about her life in Paris when she first arrived in France from Poland. She laughed, and so did Papa, when they told us how they met, bumping into each other as each carried large packages of food.

Jacqueline, my little sister, kept interrupting them with questions. "But what was in the packages? Why did Papa say it was his fault when it was really yours, Mama? Why did the cabbage roll down the hill? Why . . . "

"Will you stop it!" I said to her. "You never let anybody finish a story without interrupting. You're such a brat."

Jacqueline's eyes filled with tears. Luckily, Mama was too busy talking and laughing to notice.

"All right, all right," I told her. "Don't be such a crybaby. I didn't mean it."

"And I have a present for you," my friend Françoise said to Jacqueline. She handed Jacqueline a small box. Quickly, Jacqueline opened it.

"Oh, it's so beautiful, Françoise!" she cried, pulling a bracelet out of the box. "And it's a charm bracelet. I always wanted a charm bracelet. Look, here's a star, and a little elephant, and—oh look—a tiny bird, and a . . ."

Françoise helped her put it on. "I used to wear it when I was eight, and I loved it, too. But now I'm thirteen, like Nicole; I'm really too old. Besides, it makes me happy to give it to somebody special like you."

Jacqueline ran over to the grown-ups. She had to show it to everybody in the room, over and over again, holding out her thin little arm and jingling the bracelet.

My father kissed her head, and pulled her into his lap, where she continued to interrupt the conversation and jingle her bracelet.

"She's such a brat," I complained to Françoise.

"Oh, Nicole, you're too hard on her. She's only eight. I wish I had a little sister."

"Well, anyway, it was nice of you to give her your charm bracelet."

Françoise shrugged. "I actually have a couple more, in gold, but I thought she'd enjoy this even if it's only an inexpensive silver one."

Françoise's family was wealthy and influential in our town. But it had never gotten in the way of our friendship.

We went out on the veranda to talk.

"I'll miss you," I said. "I guess you'll be so busy in Switzerland, seeing the sights and making friends, you'll forget about me."

"I'll never have a friend like you," Françoise said. She put her arms around me, and we hugged.

"It will be over soon," I said, echoing my father, "and then you'll be back."

Her mother appeared in the doorway. "It's time to go, Françoise. Say good-bye to Nicole, and . . ."

Now it was Françoise who had tears in her eyes. "No!" she said. "I can't. Please, Mama, can Nicole stay over tonight for the last time? Please!"

"Oh, Françoise, you know how much we have to do, and we're leaving so early."

"Please!"

"No, no!" Now my mother stood next to Mme Reston. "You will have plenty of time when the war is over. Nicole, you have homework to do for school."

"I've done it, Mama. Please let me go. I mean, if Mme Reston agrees. Please! I can go on to school in the morning, and be back for lunch at noon. Please!"

Nobody said no. I gathered up my things, and Françoise and I hurried outside before the grown-ups could change their minds. As I stood at the bottom of the staircase, I heard the Restons saying good-bye to my parents, and I realized I hadn't kissed them as I usually did when I left for school. But the door to my apartment was closing, and the wedge of light that flowed out narrowed until it was gone.

I would never see them again, but how was I to know that as I happily followed Françoise out into the street?

CHAPTER 2

November 1943–March 1944
Aix-les-Bains, France

The next morning, the Restons were frantically finishing their packing as Françoise and I hugged for the last time, and I left for school. It seemed to me that nothing had changed. Outside the *Café du Nord*, some people were drinking their coffee and eating the lumpy rolls that passed for croissants. Flour had been in short supply since the war started. A woman was shaking a rug out of her window, and I caught up with some of my classmates on their way to school.

Jacqueline was not in school, but then she always managed to convince Mama that she had a sore throat or an upset stomach. Brat! I thought.

I felt sleepy as I walked home from school for lunch. Françoise and I had been up late talking. I was eager to see my mother, and to tell her all about the Restons' departure.

Nobody was home. But right in the middle of the living-room floor lay the little silver charm bracelet that Françoise had given Jacqueline. What did that mean? Maybe Jacqueline really was sick, and Mama had taken her to the doctor.

I hurried into my parents' bedroom. Nothing was in place. Every drawer in the chest had been opened and their clothes lay twisted on the floor, along with their papers and books. Over on one side was our family's photograph album with some of the pages torn out. I picked it up, and somebody cried, "Nicole! Nicole! What are you doing here?"

Behind me stood Mme Barras, our landlady.

"Where is my mother? Where is Jacqueline? What happened?"

"Hurry!" she cried. "Go away! Hide! They are looking for you."

"Who?" I cried.

"The Gestapo," she said, almost in tears. "They came in the middle of the night. They forced their way into the house. Oh, Nicole, they grabbed me and yelled, 'Where are the Jews?' I acted as if I didn't know what they were talking about, but they pushed me upstairs ahead of them, and banged on the door to your apartment." For a moment, she choked up.

"Then they . . . they . . . your father . . . he was so surprised, poor man—who would expect such a thing? They threw him against the wall, and Jacqueline, a beautiful little child like that . . . they grabbed her by the wrist and began shaking her. Then your mother, your poor mother, she got down on her hands and knees to those animals. She begged them to take her and leave Jacqueline and your father, but they kept asking where you were.

"Your father wouldn't say even though they—well, never mind what they did. He never told them where you were."

Mme Barras told me to run away, to hide, because they were looking for me. "Hurry!" she said. "Don't stay here, Nicole. They will be coming back. Hurry! Go away!"

I grabbed the photograph album and stuffed it into my book bag. She held the door open as I hurried out, but halfway down the stairs, I stopped.

"What is it?" she cried. "You can't waste any time."

But I ran back up the stairs to pick it up—the little charm bracelet that Jacqueline loved so much. I put it into my pocket, to keep it safe until I could give it back to her.

Everywhere I went, nobody wanted to help me. Many of our Jewish friends had also been taken or were in hiding. Our Christian friends were too frightened to hide me. The Gestapo had instituted a general reign of terror. Not only were Jews being arrested, but any Christian who hid Jews would also be taken, and his family as well. I wandered all over town, as one door after another was closed in my face.

Finally, exhausted, I collapsed inside the entrance to my school. I spent the night crying and half sleeping as I tried to understand what had happened.

It was cold and dark, and in between half dreams, I wondered if I should give myself up to the Gestapo. At least I would be together with my family. I kept fingering the little bracelet and thinking how happy Jacqueline would be when I gave it back to her.

My teeth were chattering and my tears had frozen on my face when Mlle Le Grand, the headmistress of our school, found me there in the morning.

"My poor child," she said. "I know what happened. Come in. Come in."

Everybody knew that Mlle Le Grand was pro-German, but she took me in and sheltered me. She said she was only doing her duty since I had been her student for many years and I was French. Later, I discovered there might have been another reason as well. She arranged for me to sleep at the boarding house connected to the school, and she treated me the same as she always had—sternly and formally. But I was grateful because she took me in when nobody else would.

SO I STAYED THERE, waiting for my family to return. Soon, I told myself, the war will be over, and they will come back—Papa, Mama, and Jacqueline.

I thought of them all the time. I had the album of pictures I found after the Gestapo looted our apartment when they took my family away. Sometimes, when I lay in bed at night, I pretended that my family came to me. After a while, their faces began to blur, and I couldn't see them clearly. I looked at their pictures in the album every day, and tried to hold on to their memory.

Mlle Le Grand, the headmistress, pretended not to notice that some of the teachers had secret radios with news from the BBC. Mlle Gerard, whose brother, we thought, was in the Underground, whispered to some of the other teachers that the Russians had broken the German siege of Leningrad. On all fronts, she whispered, the Allies were advancing. We girls heard the whispers, and whispered the news to one another. Soon it would be over. Soon there would be plenty to eat. And soon, my family would return.

Jacqueline, my little sister, came to me at night, when I lay there, shivering in the darkness. I promised her, as she slipped into bed with me, "Jacqueline, I will never make fun of you again. I have your charm bracelet and I'll give it to you when I see you again." She didn't hear me. "Tell me a story," she whispered. She always wanted me to tell her stories, and most of the time I refused. But not anymore. I began telling her a story. Then, Mama and Papa were standing there together, smiling down at me out of blurry faces. They were whispering, and I couldn't hear what they were saying.

"When?" I cried out.

They continued to whisper.

"No! No!" I pleaded, because they were slipping away, smiling. Even Jacqueline. I tried, but I couldn't hold on to her. And all I heard were whispers.

CHAPTER 3

June 7, 1944
Aix-les-Bains, France

The school is closed!" said Mlle Le Grand. She stood in front of us—students and teachers—her face immobile, her posture upright.

As the rustling and murmuring began, Mlle Le Grand clapped her hands impatiently. "You will be served lunch, and then all students must leave immediately thereafter. Within three hours, this building will be closed."

"But why?" asked Mme Chardin, our chemistry teacher. "What has happened?"

Mlle Le Grand shook her head. "I am not at liberty to discuss this further. I would like to see all the staff in my office immediately. Students should go and pack their bags. Lunch will be served in one hour."

"But where should we go?" I couldn't help crying out. I looked over at Rosette, the only other Jewish girl in the school. She also looked frightened. Most of the other girls in the boarding school had a place to go. Rosette and

I had been hiding in the school ever since the Gestapo had taken our parents away.

"Go and pack!" Mlle Le Grand ordered, ignoring my question. "During lunch, you will receive further instructions."

Little Jeanne-Marie Collard began crying, and Huguette Delaunay put an arm around her. Other girls were crying, too. I found myself shaking. It's one thing to hate school, as I often did, but it's another to be thrown out with no place to go.

Then the whispering began, and spread throughout the room. Yesterday, the Allies had landed at Normandy. The invasion of France had begun. For the Germans, it was the beginning of the end.

"Go! Pack!" Mlle Le Grand commanded. "At once!"

Bit by bit, we learned that the Germans had ordered all schools closed. They had commandeered buses, trains, and trucks. An immediate curfew was ordered that afternoon. Nobody could be out on the streets after dark— adults and children alike—or they would be shot on sight.

"What will we do?" Rosette Segal sobbed. "Where will we go?"

"Don't worry," I told her. "We'll be together, at least. Don't take much. I'll think of something."

"I haven't got much to take," Rosette said, and then suddenly we were laughing.

"Soon," I told her, "it will be over. Your parents, my parents—they'll be back."

We started packing. All I had was one other skirt, aside from the one I was wearing; two shirts, both faded; some torn underwear and stockings; and a precious wool sweater Mama had given to me when school first started.

"I saved this one," Mama said, "just for you." Her face was rosy with pleasure. "It's a fine, heavy one. And just look at the color—such a bright blue! It must have been made before the war."

"Mmm!" I said. To me, it looked babyish and clumsy.

"Nobody will have a sweater like this," Mama bubbled on, unaware of my feelings. "I found it in an old box I thought was empty. As soon as I saw it, I said to myself, 'That one is for Nicole. It's so beautiful and real wool. She'll be so happy to have it when the cold weather comes.'"

I shrugged, and Mama said, "A sweater like this could sell for lots of money."

"It's all right," I told her, and watched the pleasure ebb away from her face.

Now, as I packed it, I put my head down and kissed it before tenderly folding it so it would fit into my suitcase. All through the freezing winter, I had worn it day and night against the endless cold. "Thank you, Mama," I whispered. "I'm sorry."

"But where will we go?" Rosette asked. "I don't know anybody in this town. Do you?"

"Yes," I told her bitterly, and thought about all the friends of our family who were too frightened to protect me back in November, after the Germans had taken my parents and had threatened to arrest anybody who hid Jews. M. and Mme Bernard wouldn't even open the door when I knocked, Mme Latour said she was too sick, and the Durands suggested I hide in some other village far away so that nobody could blame them for helping a Jewish child.

"No," I said angrily, "none of them will help us."

Rosette whimpered, and I said quickly, "Don't worry. I'll think of something."

Rosette looked at me with trusting eyes. She was my age, but smaller and frail, with large eyes in a thin face. All of us were thin, but Rosette was the skinniest. She was the newest girl in the school, and had attached herself to me almost as soon as she heard I was Jewish, and that my parents had also been taken by the Germans. I didn't like her as well as Françoise, of course, but I knew I had to take care of her whether I wanted to or not.

"It will be all right," I said, smiling and nodding, although I didn't know that it would be all right, and inside me, a feeling of terrible helplessness began to grow.

"So?" I asked her. "Have you finished your packing? We need to go down for lunch. Here, let me help you."

Whispers as all of us carried our bags and suitcases down to the dining room. Terrifying whispers that the Nazis had killed everybody in a small village to the north as a reprisal because the Underground had bombed a railroad, blowing up the tracks and derailing all the trains on them. More than two hundred people, including children our age and even younger, had been rounded up and shot in front of their own church.

But the smell of food made us forget. We took our accustomed seats at the table, Rosette on my right, Huguette on my left. Mme Chardin dished out bowls of soup for everybody at our table. To our astonishment, our bowls were filled with vegetables, and even tiny wisps of what could be meat. We hadn't had such a thick soup in ages. "Probably, they are using all the supplies that were supposed to last for the rest of the month," Huguette whispered.

I stirred a recognizable piece of potato in my bowl, and breathed in the delicious fragrance. I saw chunks of carrots, cabbage, leeks, and celery. Hungry as I was, I didn't want to eat it quickly. All around me, girls were gulping down their soup. Nobody said a word.

Slowly, I lifted the potato to my mouth. I chewed it slowly, and carefully let it slide down my throat. Others had already finished their soup, and looked hungrily toward Mme Chardin. She shook her head—no seconds.

I looked down at my bowl. I avoided the eyes of my friends who had finished their own soup. I couldn't help them. This was my soup, and I would eat it slowly and not share it.

Later, as we chewed on our regular dry, coarse bread and drank our bitter coffee, Mlle Le Grand stood up and spoke.

"I am not going to say good-bye, girls," she said, "because the school will open again. The war is ending, and once peace has been established, we will all meet again. In the meantime, I am going to read out the names of each student, and ask her to stand up and join the teacher I name. She will assist you in finding your families or friends."

Mlle Le Grand read off the names on her list without pausing or commenting.

"Rosette Segal, Mme Reynard," she said finally.

Rosette turned toward me, a questioning look on her face.

"Go," I whispered. "I'll probably be next."

But I was not. One by one, each girl who was called rose and joined the teacher assigned to her.

Finally, all the tables were empty, except for mine. And only one girl was left sitting. Me.

"Nicole Nieman," recited Mlle Le Grand, looking up. "Please come with me to my office."

I hesitated, exchanging glances with Rosette and my other friends, who were being led away by their teachers.

"Nicole Nieman," said Mlle Le Grand, "I am waiting."

CHAPTER 4

Mlle Le Grand seated herself behind her desk and motioned for me to take a seat on the other side. "Where will you go?" she asked, and checked her watch.

"I don't know, *Mademoiselle*," I said, looking at her longingly.

"Don't you have friends in town—friends of your parents?"

"No!" I shook my head. "None of them would take me in when the Germans took my parents and sister. I went to all of them. One of them shut the door in my face."

"Lucky," Mlle Le Grand said, "that you were not at home when they came."

"You took me in," I said quickly. "You said it was your duty. You helped me. You . . ." I reached out a hand toward her, across the desk.

She nodded and patted my hand lightly. "Yes, Nicole, I did help you, and I helped Rosette, too. I'm glad you remember. I hope after this war ends, you will continue to remember."

"I'll always remember," I promised.

Later, when she was brought to trial for collaborating with the Germans, Rosette and I testified on her behalf, and she was not imprisoned. But then, on the day the school closed, I hoped only that she would help me as she had before.

"Good," she nodded approvingly. "But now, where will you go?"

"I was hoping, *Mademoiselle,* that you could . . . you could . . ."

"Impossible, Nicole," she said. Her voice suddenly shook, and she bit her lip. "I'm not sure where I will be going, and I can't help you now. I can't." She was afraid, I realized. This strong, cold woman whom I had always considered unmoved by anything, was frightened.

"I never thought," she said almost to herself, "it would end this way."

"But didn't you hope it would end this way?" I asked, puzzled.

"I didn't want the Germans to stay here. It was humiliating that they were able to conquer France so easily, and I certainly did not admire some of their practices—especially toward the Jews. But I did admire their strength, and I did hope that *Maréchal Pétain* would be able to restore the former glory of France. But perhaps I misunderstood."

She looked at her watch again. "We need to be out of here within an hour. Nicole, you must go somewhere. Don't you have an aunt?"

"An aunt!" I repeated disdainfully.

"Yes, an aunt—your father's sister, I believe."

"She isn't—well, she was never very interested in me," I mumbled. "And besides, the first thing she did when they took my parents was to leave town and go into hiding."

"Now, Nicole," lectured Mlle Le Grand, "compose yourself. This is no time to speak so disrespectfully of your elders. I'm afraid you forget yourself from time to time. Even your poor mother was concerned about your behavior."

"My mother had no respect for my aunt. She said that my aunt never accepted any responsibilities. She said—"

"I don't think we need to go into family arguments at this point."

I remained silent.

"Nicole, I am speaking to you. Do you know where she is? Please answer me."

"Yes, *Mademoiselle,* I know where she is, but I don't like her. She broke my mother's beautiful glass vase. She—"

"Where is she, Nicole?"

Reluctantly, I pulled out a card from my suitcase. It said, "I am fine. Remember, I am here in Gap." It was signed "Raymonde." I handed it to Mlle Le Grand.

"Raymonde?" she asked, surprised.

"That's not her real name. Her real name is Sophie Nieman."

Mlle Le Grand turned the card over and examined it. "She gives no return address."

"That's just like her," I said impatiently. "How could I find her, even if I wanted to?"

Mlle Le Grand handed the card back to me. "That's exactly what you will have to do." She stood up. "Do you have any money?"

"A little."

She put her hand into the pocket of her dress, and handed me some francs. "Now, go!" she said. "You can take the bus to Chambéry, and then the train to Grenoble. There is another bus from there to Gap."

"But *Mademoiselle* . . ."

"Go!" she said. "Now!"

I rose, but then hesitated. "Rosette?" I asked. "What about Rosette?"

"Mme Reynard will see that Rosette is in safe hands."

"But, *Mademoiselle,* I promised I would look after her. I told her not to worry."

Mlle Le Grand shook her head. "Do you think, Nicole, that you are the only one who can handle matters? This is a real flaw in your character—that you think you are superior to adults. You must make an effort to improve yourself."

"But *Mademoiselle,* just tell me where she is."

"Go!" said Mlle Le Grand. "I am running out of patience."

I HAD NEVER SEEN as many people on the streets as I did that day. Most of them were German soldiers, heading north. Some trucks were filled with soldiers, and others with supplies. No whispers now. Loud voices shouting orders in German. Others questioning. The markets were closed, but some French people were scurrying along quickly, trying to appear inconspicuous.

In my mind, I repeated over and over again the route to Gap. Take a bus to Chambéry, which was fifteen kilometers away, then a train to Grenoble, one hundred kilometers, then a bus to Gap. I focused on it, like a chant to allay the sick fear inside me. Over and over I said it—a bus to Chambéry, the train to Grenoble. I tried not to think about how I would be able to buy tickets when the Germans had commandeered all the buses and trains.

But, at first, it was easy. Few people were heading south. It was no problem buying a ticket to Chambéry, not far from Aix-les-Bains. I sat by myself in the station, hoping that anybody who noticed me would see only a fourteen-year-old schoolgirl, probably on her way home. The trip took fifteen minutes, so I didn't have much time to worry.

It was much harder buying a ticket from Chambéry to Grenoble, a large city where German forces were stationed. I stood in a line, behind a group of German soldiers, and tried to look calm. If anybody found out I was Jewish, I knew I wouldn't have a chance.

"No! No! No!" said the stationmaster when I reached the counter. "There are no seats left. Only German soldiers are permitted on the train."

"But, *Monsieur*," I pleaded. "I must go to Grenoble. I must! It's an emergency."

The stationmaster said impatiently, "Everything is an emergency, nowadays. Everybody has a story. Everybody has an emergency. I just told you that there are no more tickets. Didn't you hear what I had to say? Now go away!"

I couldn't contain myself. I cried. The tears rolled down my face. "My grandmother," I wept, "Oh, my grandmother!" Actually, both of my grandmothers lived in Poland, but I was filled with an overwhelming misery and helplessness, so it didn't matter what I said.

"Oh, give her a ticket," came a voice behind me, in broken French. "Some of my buddies aren't coming, so you should have enough seats, particularly for a young girl whose grandmother is sick. You sound so heartless."

The stationmaster's nasty expression turned so quickly it seemed like magic. Suddenly, he was smiling and almost bowing. "Certainly, *Monsieur,* if you say so. Certainly. I meant no harm. Now, *Mademoiselle,* here you are. Here is your ticket. Did you want it one-way or round-trip? Either way. Whatever you say."

I turned, the tears still wet on my face. A smiling German soldier stood behind me. I felt sick to my stomach, thinking I would have to thank a German soldier, maybe even one who had taken away my family. I wept even harder.

"Now, now," the soldier said, patting my shoulder. "Don't cry! I'm sorry about your grandmother, but you'll be home in no time. Here, let me carry your suitcase."

So I didn't have to thank him then. He led me onto the train, and put my suitcase up on the rack above my seat. He chatted away in clumsy French, telling me what a beautiful country France was. He said that, when the war ended, he hoped to come back and visit the Loire Valley, where all the historic buildings and castles are. He said he was studying history in college and hoped to finish his studies after the war.

I remained silent, but he didn't notice. After he put my suitcase on the rack, he wished me good luck, and then rejoined some other German soldiers, sitting a few seats away. They spoke to him in German, and he replied in German. They were laughing, and soon he was laughing, too.

Over the hour it took to reach Grenoble, I looked at him quickly from time to time. He was young, maybe a few years older than me, and he acted like an ordinary young man, maybe going on a pleasure trip. He didn't seem like an invader who might have taken away my family and other Jewish families. Not like somebody who might have shot over two hundred men, women, and children in that small town up north. Not like somebody who might have shot me if he had known that I was Jewish.

CHAPTER 5

June 8, 1944
Gap, France

I reached Grenoble late in the afternoon. The German soldier took down my suitcase, and asked if he could help me in any other way.

"No, no!" I said quickly. And even though it hurt, I added, "Thank you."

"Good-bye," he said. "I hope your grandmother recovers." Then he rejoined his companions.

I waited until the platform was empty before asking directions to the bus station.

Again, it was no problem buying a ticket to Gap, another small town in the south. The bus was only half-filled, but it stopped in every village on the way. One tire blew out, and then there was a problem with the bus driver, who suddenly had such an attack of indigestion that he needed to lie down somewhere. It took over an hour to find a replacement.

We had left Grenoble at nine that evening, but we didn't arrive in Gap until nearly seven the next morning. I tried to sleep, but I couldn't. I had time to think—about the German soldier, about Mlle Le Grand, about Rosette. Where was she? Who was there to take care of her? Was she safe, or had she also been set adrift to find help? And finally, I thought about my aunt. How was I ever going to find her? And if I did, what then?

When I finally got off the bus, I felt exhausted, rumpled, and stiff. In the washroom at the station, I washed my face and hands, combed my hair, and tried to smooth out my wrinkled clothing. I also tried smiling in the mirror.

But what did I have to smile about? I wanted my mother, I wanted my father, I even wanted my little sister, Jacqueline. How could I smile when I didn't know where they were, and how they were being treated? And here I was in a strange town, looking for an aunt I didn't even like. I looked at the smiling face in the mirror and knew that soon, it would be a crying face. But I couldn't waste time feeling sorry for myself.

I gritted my teeth and picked up my suitcase. It wouldn't be long now, I comforted myself. The war will be over, and they'll be home; then my aunt could go her way and we would go ours.

I stepped out of the washroom and looked around. It was a warm, steamy day. I opened the collar of my shirt. What now? The town was coming awake. Shopkeepers were opening their stores, children cried behind open windows, men and women hurried along the street, a postman bicycled by.

How would I ever find my aunt? Where do you go first to find a person in an unfamiliar town—even a small one like Gap? You go to the police station. No, you don't, not nowadays! You go to a synagogue if she's Jewish. No, you don't! Maybe a post office. A post office!

I began running. *"Monsieur! Monsieur!"* I yelled.

He kept bicycling.

"M. le facteur!" I yelled, even louder. "Please stop! Please!"

The postman stopped, slid one foot down from his pedal, and looked back at me.

"Are you calling me?" he asked, as I came puffing up.

"Yes, *Monsieur,* yes. Please. I'm trying to find my aunt."

"Did you lose her?" he asked, laughing at his own joke.

I smiled and tried to look agreeable. "Not exactly, but I haven't seen her since the war started, and we've . . . we've been separated."

"Ah, and what is her name?"

I showed him the card. He turned it over. "There's no address. There's no last name," he said. He shrugged his shoulders and handed me back the card. "You need a detective, not a mailman!" He began to get back on his bike.

"Please," I said, "she has brown hair."

He smiled. "That's a real clue."

"And she must be"—I counted on my fingers—"about forty years old."

He adjusted his mailbag on the bike, and sat back on the seat.

"And she speaks French with a funny accent."

The postman took his foot off the pedal, and wrinkled up his face. "Does she live with another woman—kind of . . . ?" He moved his hands to indicate a woman who was well shaped.

"Maybe. She has one friend who's fat."

"Oh, no," the mailman insisted. "She's not fat, she's just very well endowed." He smiled.

He got off his bike.

"I think I can help you, young lady." He pointed with his finger up a very steep street. "Go to the top of that street, and then turn left onto Rue Pasteur. Go to the end of the street, and the last house, a yellow one, is the one you will probably find your aunt in. What did you say her name was?"

"Raymonde."

"Yes, and her friend's name is Louise."

"Maybe."

"I'm pretty sure it is. And I would appreciate it if you . . . if you would give Louise my best regards, and tell her not to forget . . . to meet me in the park on Saturday at noon—near the grandstand."

He touched his cap, got back on his bike, and rode off.

I FOUND THE HOUSE. I rang the bell. A plump blond woman opened the door, and looked at me with suspicion.

"Does Raymonde live here, *Madame*?"

"Who wants her?" the woman demanded.

"Me," I said.

"And who are you?"

"Her niece, Nicole Nieman."

"Wait here," she told me, and shut the door.

In another few minutes, the door opened. My aunt, in her bathrobe, stood there blinking at me. "Nicole!" she said. "What are you doing here?" She seemed surprised; not happy, just surprised.

"They closed the school," I told her, "and my head-mistress told me to come here. I had no other place to go."

For a moment, she didn't move. Finally, she put an arm around my shoulder and kissed me lightly on my cheek. "Of course," she said. "Come in, Nicole! How are you? Are you hungry? Are you thirsty? How did you get here? How did you find me? Have you heard from your parents?" Her questions went on and on, but before I could begin answering them, I had a message to deliver. I turned to the plump blond woman and asked, "Is your name Louise?"

"Yes," she said. "It is."

"The postman—I don't know his name—sent his best regards, and said I should tell you not to forget to meet him in the park on Saturday, at noon, near the grand-stand."

"Oh, him," said Louise, laughing. "I guess he'll do for the time being."

CHAPTER 6

August 20, 1944,
Gap, France

Early that morning, not much later than daybreak, a
man on a motorcycle rode through the quiet streets,
shouting, "*Les Américains arrivent! Les Américains
arrivent!*"

I was the first to open the window and see him as he
sped along the street. Other windows also opened, and
voices called out, "What did he say?" "Did he really say
that the Americans have come?" "When did he say they
would arrive?" "Do you believe him?"

Soon Louise and my aunt joined me at the window,
shouting to their neighbors and laughing.

In the past few days, we had been listening continually
to the BBC. We knew that Allied forces had landed in
Toulon from North Africa, and were moving swiftly north.
But we were unprepared for such a rapid advance. Most of
us had stayed indoors for the few preceding days, watching
from our windows as German soldiers hurried south helter-
skelter, obviously unprepared for the invasion.

The empty streets filled rapidly as people spilled out of their houses. Many of them were still in bathrobes. There was no sign of the Germans now. Only a rumbling sound in the distance that grew louder and louder.

And then they came.

First, a tank with American soldiers standing up. Smiling American soldiers waving to us and speaking in English.

The streets filled with all our neighbors, cheering, laughing, crying, reaching up to touch their hands.

"*Bienvenus!*" most of the people cried, but I, who had studied English for four years, could yell proudly, "Welcome! *Messieurs!* Welcome!"

Other tanks followed, and then soldiers on foot. Some stopped to laugh and hand out Chiclets and pieces of chocolate to the crowd. Nobody refused either the chocolate or the Chiclets. Most of us had eaten no chocolate in the past few years. We accepted both happily, even though nobody knew what, exactly, to do with the Chiclets. One of the soldiers demonstrated to us how to chew them. It was hard to manage without swallowing. Nobody was silent.

"Are you really here to stay?"

"Where are the Germans?"

"Please don't go away."

Most of the soldiers couldn't speak French, and I tried to speak to them in English. But Mlle Le Grand had taught us never to speak a sentence unless it is grammatically correct. The verb always has to agree with the subject.

My aunt shoved her way to the front of the crowd. She was sobbing and laughing at the same time. She embraced every soldier she could reach, jabbering away at them in her funny French, in Polish, and finally Yiddish.

"*Ich vershteh,*" one soldier said to her in Yiddish.

"*Oy,*" said my aunt. "*Bist du a Yid?*"

No, the soldier explained, laughing, he was not Jewish. He was of Italian extraction, but he had grown up in a Jewish neighborhood in New York City, and his best friend was Jewish. So he could understand Yiddish, and even speak a little.

My aunt was overjoyed. "What can we do for you?" she cried in Yiddish. "Anything! We're so grateful you've come. Please, tell us what we can do."

Finally, the soldier said they had eaten only dried rations for weeks, and if she, if anybody, could give him and some of his friends any fresh food—an egg, butter, cheese—that would be like heaven.

My aunt shook her head, and was silent for a short second or two. That was about all the time my aunt could ever be silent.

"Oh, that's all right," the soldier said, seeing her embarrassment. "We don't need a reward for winning this victory so easily. That's really the best reward."

"No, no," my aunt insisted. "Please, come to my home in a few hours—here's my address—and we'll have a real meal for you and your friends."

She traded a gold bracelet and a pair of shoes to a farmer for a dozen eggs and a small pot of butter. The baker in town lit his oven and made the best kind of bread he could from the coarse, blended flour.

All over the town, others rounded up any fresh vegetables they could find, small pieces of meat, and dried fish, and cooked al fresco meals, while the American soldiers sat on stones in the street, eating whatever was offered them, and laughing and talking with their French hosts.

My aunt cooked an omelet for about ten soldiers. We stood around them on the street, serving, but eating nothing ourselves. The aroma of the fresh eggs was dizzying. None of us had eaten eggs for many months. One of the Americans gave me a brass button from his uniform. It said "US" on it, and every day, I rubbed it and rubbed it, until it shone like gold.

OVER THE NEXT FEW DAYS, we watched as the Americans moved into the town. They brought more tanks, more supply trucks, and, finally, the German prisoners. They marched through the town with armed American guards on either side of them. Their heads were bowed, and they avoided looking at us directly.

"*Sales boches! Sales boches!*" people screamed. They cursed them, and threw rocks. I did too, screaming and demanding that they give me back my family. The Americans tried to stop us.

"Now, folks," they kept saying, "move back. It's all right. They're our prisoners, and we're going to make sure they won't hurt anybody. Just move back, and let us pass."

But still, people threw rocks and cursed and spit at them. Some of the Germans' faces were bloodied, and others cried like children.

There had been no resistance, we heard. The German soldiers had not fought as they had up at Normandy, where the Allies had finally broken through and were on their way to Paris. Here, the Germans, confused and disorganized, had simply thrown down their arms and surrendered. These mighty conquerors of the world, being paraded along the streets with their bloodied faces and tears, were now the conquered.

NOBODY SLEPT for the next few days. It felt like an endless party, and it was. For me, I knew now that the war was finally, really coming to an end, and that my parents and little sister soon would be returning home.

CHAPTER 7

September 20, 1944
Aix-les-Bains, France

Within a few weeks, my aunt and I had returned to
Aix-les-Bains.

The war was practically over in France. On
August 25, Allied forces had entered Paris. In other parts
of Europe, the war continued to rage, but here in Aix-les-
Bains, we were free.

Our town struggled to restore law and order. The
Underground had surfaced and was meting out justice in
its own way. All known informers were rounded up and
shot in the streets. One of them had informed on my own
parents and other Jewish families in the town, drawing up
lists and handing them over to the Gestapo.

I saw none of the killings, only piles of sand that had
been heaped over the blood of the dead men.

Women who had been lovers of German soldiers were
publicly humiliated by having the hair shaved off their
heads and being paraded around in front of jeering crowds.

"Look, over there!" I said to my aunt. "There is M. Thibaut. His sister is one of the women the crowd is jeering at. He is making the most noise. But he was always hanging around the Nazis, running errands for them and joking with them. Why should he get away with it?"

My aunt shrugged and put on more lipstick. We were watching from the veranda of the apartment on the Avenue du Petit Port where I had lived with my parents before the Germans took them away. My aunt's boyfriend, Henri Sarmian, was moving in with us that evening. My aunt had a table set up on the veranda, covered with my mother's old handmade lace tablecloth. It was stained on one side by the tenants who had lived there after my parents were taken. They had used not only the tablecloth, but all the other linens that remained in the old linen closet, as well as any of the furniture that the Germans had not broken.

These tenants had been acceptable to the German authorities, and it took us a while to convince them to leave. I finally suggested that we ask the Underground to help settle the dispute, at which point they quickly departed.

"It's all over," my aunt said. "Now, the good times are coming. Nicole, why don't you sweep up around the apartment before Henri arrives, and make sure there is a towel for him in the bathroom, and perhaps you could run down to the *crémerie* and see if they have any cheese."

That's when I knew for sure that I did not want to live with my aunt. Even though my father was her brother, it seemed as if she had forgotten all about him and the rest of my family. She wanted to have the kind of fun I knew my family would never have approved of.

"No," I said. "They do not have any cheese. You sent me there yesterday, and Mlle Jeanette said it would be weeks, maybe months before they would have any kind of decent cheese."

"Oh, well, you never know," said my aunt. She held up a hand mirror before her face, and began combing her hair. "Nicole, why don't you see if you can find some flowers for the table? Mme Frenay has some pretty pink and purple ones growing in her yard. I'm sure she'll give you some if you ask her."

"No," I said. "I'm not going to ask her. And I don't think it's right that you have a man coming to stay here when Mama and Papa and Jacqueline will be coming home any day now."

My aunt stopped looking at herself in the mirror and said, surprised, "Why are you so angry, Nicole? Of course, Henri and I will go someplace else when they return. But in the meantime"—her eyes moved around the veranda and through the open doors to the rest of the apartment—"we should fix it up for them. Everything looks so shabby. And we do need more furniture—a new bed in my room, and in yours." Suddenly, she laughed. "Henri is very handy. As soon as we can, he should paint the whole apartment—maybe blue in the living room, peach in my bedroom, white in the kitchen and bathroom, and . . . whatever color you like in your bedroom."

"No!" I insisted. "No! We have to wait until my family comes home. They should be the ones who decide. We shouldn't make any changes until they return. No!"

I knew that my tone was disrespectful, but it didn't seem to bother my aunt. She changed the subject and began speaking about the menu for dinner that night. "How lucky I was to find a chicken! And did I tell you, Nicole, that Louise and a new friend of hers will also join us for dinner?"

"No," I said, "you didn't tell me. Anyway, I think I'll take a walk."

"Good," said my aunt. "Some fresh air will cheer you up. And remember to ask Mme Frenay for some flowers."

I STORMED OUT OF THE HOUSE. No! I thought. I can't stay here with her. All she and her friends think about is parties. They don't want me around, and I don't want to be with them, either. The apartment belongs to my family, not to her and her silly friends. I need to go somewhere else, but where?

I hurried along the street and found myself heading automatically in the direction of my school. The door was open. Mlle Le Grand! Maybe she's back, I thought. Maybe she'll let me stay here at school. I'd rather stay with her than with my aunt.

I ran up the stairs and into her office. She was bending down, rearranging a file behind her desk.

"Mlle Le Grand!" I cried. "You've come back."

She turned and smiled. It was not Mlle Le Grand.

"I am Mme Marchand," she said. "And who are you?"

"My name is Nicole Nieman. I am a student here, but when Mlle Le Grand closed the school, I had to—"

"Yes, I know," she said kindly. "Please sit down."

"Where is Mlle Le Grand?" I asked. "Is she safe?"

Mme Marchand said, "She is safe, but no longer headmistress. I am your new headmistress, and I look forward to meeting all of my students. I have been checking the records of those students who lived in the boardinghouse here. All the others found safe places to hide, but I was concerned about you. Did you find your aunt? Are you both back here in Aix-les-Bains? Have you found a place to live?"

"Yes, *Madame,* but, you see, it is the apartment my parents had. My aunt and . . . and a friend of hers are living there. I'm waiting for my parents to return, and in the meantime, I would like to stay here as I did when the Germans took them."

Mme Marchand leaned forward. "And your aunt? How would she feel about you living here?"

"She will probably be delighted," I said bitterly. "She's so busy with her boyfriend and her other friends, I'm sure she considers me a nuisance."

Mme Marchand sighed. "Of course, she will have to agree, but if she does, there should be no problem if you stay at the boarding school. Now that the war is over here, many of the girls will want to live with their families. We should have plenty of room, and I'm sure I can arrange a scholarship for you."

"Tonight?" I asked eagerly. "Can I come immediately?"

Mme Marchand laughed. "I wish all students were as eager to return to school as you seem to be. But . . ." She shook her head. "We're not ready to open. We have some changes to make, and it should be a couple of weeks, at least, before we can."

"I could help," I urged. "I could do anything you need. I could wash windows, and I could—"

She shook her head. "Soon," she said.

I suppose my desperately unhappy face stirred her memory. She began shuffling around some papers. "I believe there was somebody who was inquiring after you. Let me see . . . ah, here is . . . another classmate of yours. She pulled out a piece of paper and read, "Rosette Segal and her mother . . ."

"Her mother?"

"Yes, her mother. They have inquired several times for your whereabouts. I know they would be happy to hear from you."

"Oh, where is she, *Madame?* I'm so happy she found her mother. I'm so eager to see her—to see them both."

Mme Marchand gave me Rosette's address. I jumped up and hurried from the room. "I will see you soon, Nicole," she called after me. "Good luck!"

I FOUND ROSETTE AT HOME. We hugged and kissed each other, and she introduced me to her mother. Rosette hung on to her mother as if she could never let go of her. Her thin little face was no longer mournful, and I listened as both of them talked at the same time about how Mme Segal had escaped and how she had hidden out with brave, sympathetic Christian friends near Aix-les-Bains. She had been unable to let her daughter know that she was safe because it would have been too risky, not only for herself, but for her friends as well.

I felt happy being with them. Perhaps the same thing had happened to my family. Seeing them together made me feel my turn was coming next. Rosette's father had still not returned, but they were sure he soon would.

Over and over again, Mme Segal thanked me for my kindness to Rosette at school. She kept repeating how eager she was to do anything she could to repay me.

"Anything!" she kept saying.

"Perhaps," I said shyly, "perhaps . . ."

"What? Just tell me."

"Perhaps," I said, "I could stay here for dinner tonight and sleep over."

CHAPTER 8

September 1944–January 1946
Aix-les-Bains, France

So I waited for them to return. All through the rest of the year, and the next year, I waited.

The war ended in Europe in May 1945. Others returned. Slowly, groups of men and women who had been held in concentration camps began arriving. Rosette's father came back in the fall of 1945. His sparse hair was completely white and many of his teeth were gone. He could hardly walk, and his body was stooped and skeletal. "I am one of the lucky ones," he said.

The Russians had liberated him from a small concentration camp in Poland, where he had been sent because of his skill as a carpenter. He had been in a hospital for months after the liberation until he regained enough strength to be put on a train and return home.

He had stories, terrible stories, about atrocities committed by the Nazis in the concentration camps—mass killings, torture, beatings, and always hunger and cold.

Mme Segal kept him in bed for a couple of weeks, and fed him all the food she could get her hands on. Friends helped with gifts of fruit, fish, and bread that had begun tasting like bread again.

I TRIED NOT TO LISTEN to the horror stories that the streams of refugees told. I continued to believe that my family would return; that they had escaped the savagery that M. Segal and others related.

Now I lived at school, and it was a different place under Mme Marchand. There was laughter, kindness, and no fear. There was food—not the delicious cheeses and meat and cakes I vaguely remembered from before the war, but as supplies continued to grow, we ate enough food to fill us up.

Mme Marchand and her husband had belonged to the Underground. They had two children: a grown son and a daughter who also taught at the school. Mme Marchand knew all of her students, especially the thirty girls who boarded at the school. Rosette no longer lived there, but she attended classes during the day. She lived with her family, and often, I was invited to join them.

I felt related to them in a way I never felt with my own aunt. I hardly spent time with her. She had painted the apartment in colors that were cheap and garish, and she had bought showy furniture and hung silly pictures on the wall. It no longer looked

like home, and I knew my parents would change everything around as soon as they arrived home.

Mme Marchand asked our opinions. She said
her door was always open if any of us wished to speak
with her.

As ever, I had many opinions.

One day, Huguette, Marie, Suzanne, and I stood quietly in front of her desk.

She looked up, smiled at us, and asked, "Is there anything special you wanted to speak to me about?"

"Yes, *Madame,*" I answered. I was always the one
who spoke up.

"Yes, what is it?"

"You see, *Madame,* none of us have ever—the school
has never allowed us—to go to the movies. Now that the
movie theater has reopened, it is showing a film we would
like to see."

"And what is it, may I ask?"

"It's *La Belle et la Bête,* by Jean Cocteau. We hear
from our friends that it is a very artistic film, and not at
all offensive."

Mme Marchand thought it over while we stood
there, and then she shrugged. "Why not?" she said. "But
I will ask one of the teachers to chaperone you."

"Thank you, *Madame,*" we all said.

"You're welcome!" said Mme Marchand. "And remember that I am always happy to hear your opinions."

SHE MAY HAVE REGRETTED her interest in my opinions because I had so many. Another day, I stood there with seven girls.

"Yes, Nicole, what is it now?"

"Well, you see, *Madame,* some of us older girls feel we have too much homework. We all study Latin, Greek, French literature, math, chemistry, and physics, as well as music and art."

"And?"

"For most of us, we have at least seventy-two hours of homework. There's hardly any time left to do anything else. We feel it is too much."

"I will look into it, Nicole."

"Thank you, *Madame.*"

"You're welcome, Nicole."

Shortly afterward, our homework had shrunk to about forty hours. Some of the teachers had sullen faces, and one even called me the ringleader.

Another day, eleven of us stood in Mme Marchand's office.

"What is it this time, Nicole?"

"Some of us, *Madame,* feel that there should be more separation in the dormitories. We feel that the younger girls should have one dormitory floor to themselves, and that we teenage girls should have a dormitory of our own. There are many reasons why, *Madame,* and if you wish, I can state them."

"That won't be necessary, Nicole. I agree with you, and will see that the changes will take place."

"Thank you, *Madame*."

"You're welcome, Nicole."

ROSETTE'S FAMILY HAD decided to emigrate to the United States. Once the war was over, Mme Segal's brother, who lived in the United States, filled out all the necessary papers for her, and she hoped that she and her family would be able to leave within six months.

"I only wish you were coming," Rosette said.

By now, we had become best friends.

Mme Segal asked me many times if I wanted to go.

"Do you have any relatives in America?" she asked.

"I think there are some cousins of my father in New York, and I know that my mother has an aunt somewhere. But no, I don't want to go to America. I want to be here when my parents return."

"Of course," said Mme Segal. "Of course, but . . ."

I waited for her to finish her sentence, but she did not. Instead, she said, "Of course we will be in touch with you, and if you—and your family—want to come, I will see what I can do."

"Oh, no, *Madame*," I said. "I'm sure they will want to stay here."

CHAPTER 9

May 1946
Aix-les-Bains, France

He came on a day in May, when Suzanne and I were looking in the mirror at our images and arguing about who was prettier. She said I was, and I said she was. Both of us, I think, believed the opposite.

"You have blond hair and bright blue eyes," I told her.

"My teeth stick out," she said, opening her mouth. "Yours are straighter."

"And you have a cute little nose."

"But your mouth is smaller."

Mlle Marchand, the headmistress's daughter, who taught math at our school, suddenly appeared behind us in the mirror.

"Both of you are ugly," she laughed, making a hideous face that embarrassed Suzanne and me. "Anyway, Nicole, somebody wants to see you downstairs. He's in my mother's office."

"I'll go," I said to Suzanne. "But I'll be right back, so wait for me."

Mme Marchand was not in her office—only an old, sickly looking man, who stood up when I entered the room.

"I'm sorry," he said. "I meant to come earlier, but my family didn't let me. You see, I was sick, and then I caught pneumonia."

I shook my head. I didn't know him.

"You are Nicole Nieman, aren't you?"

"Yes, *Monsieur,*" I said with a questioning look, "but I don't know you, do I?"

"No, you don't," he said. "My name is Louis Kaplan." He looked at me thoughtfully. "You look so much like him," he said in a low voice.

I knew before he said anything else, and I began crying.

"I'm sorry," he said. "I'm sorry." He collapsed into the chair, exhausted.

"My father," I cried, "my father . . . he's not . . . not . . . ?"

"No," he said. "He's not coming back. But he thought of you up to the end. He said how much he loved you, and your mother and your sister."

"And my mother," I sobbed, "my mother . . . is she . . . coming back?"

"No," he whispered.

By now I could hardly speak. "My sister?" I gasped. "My . . . my sister . . . my little sister?"

He shook his head.

Then Mme Marchand was there, holding me in her arms, rocking me, and stroking my head as he spoke.

All of them had been taken to Auschwitz, the infamous concentration camp in Poland. The women and children were killed immediately in the gas chambers. But the men—the strong ones—had been kept to work as slave laborers. My father had lived and worked at Auschwitz for over a year, M. Kaplan told us. The two of them had met there and had become friends.

M. Kaplan was crying now, too, as he spoke haltingly about January of 1945. The Russians were advancing, and the Germans decided to evacuate the camp. They gave their prisoners a choice of remaining in the camp or of leaving with their German captors, who were on their way back to Germany.

Most of the prisoners believed that those who chose to remain would be killed, while those who decided to leave had, at least, a chance of being liberated by the Russians. My father, M. Kaplan said, was already very weak, with a bad leg. He chose to go, and so did M. Kaplan. For my father, it was the wrong choice. He couldn't keep up with the other prisoners, and he was shot by a German guard along the road. Many others were killed as well, during what became a death march, with the bodies of murdered men lining the roadside.

Those who chose to remain were not killed, probably because the Germans were in too great a hurry to care. Those prisoners were liberated by Russian forces, who saw that they were cared for until they could return to their families.

As for himself, M. Kaplan said, he and others had managed to slip away as more and more of the German soldiers deserted.

OVER AND OVER AGAIN, I asked if he was sure, begging him to give me some kind of hope that my family or some of them or even one of them was still alive.

M. Kaplan said he had witnessed the murder of my father.

"But my mother and sister . . . ," I cried. "They could have escaped. Mme Segal, she escaped. Maybe you didn't know, maybe . . ."

He shook his head as he struggled to rise from the chair.

"If you would like," Mme Marchand said to him, "we can put you up here for the night."

"No, no, I thank you." M. Kaplan managed finally to rise from the chair. "I have a friend in town. I can go there."

He stood looking at me, crying and shivering in Mme Marchand's arms. "What can I do?" he asked helplessly. "Maybe I shouldn't have come, but he cried out to me when they pulled him out, he begged me, he . . ."

I didn't hear anything else. Mme Marchand took me home with her that night and sat by the bed until I fell asleep.

THE NEXT MORNING, I decided to go to America.

CHAPTER 10

September 1947
Bronx, New York City

My cousin Jake looked nothing like my father. As we rode uptown on the subway, he chatted away in English that I could hardly understand.

Something about a party at his house for me—how everybody was looking forward to meeting me, how happy he was I finally managed to come to America. Every so often, he patted me on the shoulder, but never paused long enough for me to respond.

Just as well! None of the English I had learned in school—"How do you do?" "I am fine." "I hope you are well." "What is your name?" "How old are you?"—seemed adequate for this bewildering day.

And then this strange, rattling train that jerked, started, and stopped while huge numbers of people rushed in or out. The unfamiliar sounds and smells—the heat and the fans churning away overhead!

He carried my suitcases as we left the station, climbed the stairs, and emerged into the light.

"Here we are," he said. "The Bronx, your new home."

I shrank next to him as we moved along the street. All those people and cars and noise! Nothing like my small town with its low houses and quiet streets.

Jake led me into a high building with an elevator. "We're on the seventh floor," he said, motioning for me to get into it.

I'd never seen an elevator before, and the terror in my eyes made him laugh.

"Come on, Nicole, nothing to be afraid of. You'll get used to it."

I did what I was told, watched him press a button, and felt the floor beneath me drop. I must have grabbed him in a panic because he mumbled something comforting.

When he opened the door to his apartment, I saw many strange people smiling at me.

"Now, Nicole," Jake said, "these are your cousins and friends of the family. Here," he said, motioning to a large, unsmiling woman, "is my wife, your cousin Harriet, and here is Sonia, my oldest daughter. She's just presented us with our first grandson, Leo." He paused, put an arm around Sonia and kissed her forehead. Sonia, a pretty blond woman, smiled at me. She was holding a tiny infant wrapped in a blue blanket. "Just look at him," Jake continued, taking the baby away from her and bouncing him up and down. "He's the image of me."

"Oh, Dad, stop it. He'll throw up," Sonia protested, laughing. "And stop spoiling him. He just bought him a tricycle," she explained to the group.

The conversation moved on to the subject of babies and grandparents. Until somebody said to me, "I'm Evvie."

"Evvie?" I repeated.

"I'm his youngest daughter," she said bitterly. "And he never knows I'm around."

At least that's what I thought she said. But then, one of the other cousins approached me and began speaking. I couldn't quite understand what she said, but when she motioned to a table spread with food, I understood what that meant.

I had never seen so much food spread out on a table before in my whole life. Some of it I couldn't identify. There were meats, fish, breads, rolls with holes in them, potato salad, cabbage salad, fruits, cakes and cookies—so many cakes and cookies, it was hard to choose. I stood there bewildered, unable to make a decision.

Somebody laughed and filled up a plate for me, handed me a fork, and said something pleasant. Who was it? So much food and so many cousins, talking and laughing together, and eating, on this, my first day in America! I ate everything on my plate. It all tasted so good, and I was hungry.

Each cousin spoke to me for a little while. They said how happy they were to see me. They said how sad they were because my family had died at Auschwitz. They all invited me to come to visit them, and then all of them talked to each other. None of them spoke French. They spoke so quickly in English I couldn't understand most of what they said.

Many of the women wore colorful dresses, and bright lipstick on their mouths. They looked well fed, happy, and unaware of what the war had done to us in Europe. I felt out of place with them, and older.

FINALLY, EVERYBODY WENT HOME, and Evvie and I ended up sitting in her bedroom, looking at each other. Like her mother, she was heavy and unsmiling. She seemed angry.

"Nobody even told me you were coming until a week ago," she said. "Nobody ever is interested in my opinion."

"Pardon?"

"Listen!" She leaned toward me, and spoke in an angry whisper. "Just because we're cousins doesn't mean we have to like each other."

She held up one finger of her hand, and slowly drew it across the room. On one side was her bed, her chest, a desk and chair, and the window, overlooking the Grand Concourse in the Bronx. On the other side was Sonia's former bed, which would now be mine, a matching chest, a chair, no desk, and the door to the rest of the apartment.

"From now on," she said, "you stay on your side of the room, and don't come over to my side. I'm going to be studying, so don't play the radio. It's on my side anyway. And don't make any noise. If I have a friend over, you'll just have to get lost."

"Lost?" I repeated, confused.

"I thought you spoke good English," she snapped. "You don't really understand anything, do you?"

I knew enough to feel her anger and scorn. Without my language, I was helpless and frightened.

I hurried out of the room, into the kitchen, where Jake stood at the sink, stirring something in a glass.

"Ah, Nicole." He smiled. "It was a big day for you, wasn't it?"

"Yes, *Monsieur*," I said.

"No, no!" He shook his head. "You call me 'Cousin Jake,' and you call my wife 'Cousin Harriet,' and all your younger cousins by their first names. The older ones, just put 'Cousin' in front of their names."

He seemed kind and agreeable, unlike Evvie.

"You must be tired," he continued. "You should go to bed." He yawned. "I'm exhausted, and tomorrow I have to go to work early. You probably won't see me until after supper, but Harriet will take care of you. Too bad Evvie has to go to school, but she'll show you around another day. Isn't it nice that you're both the same age, seventeen? I know you'll get along just fine. Of course, if Sonia were free, she'd really be the one to show you around. She knows how to have fun."

"So . . ." He stood there awkwardly, and then reached out and patted my shoulder. "Good night, Nicole, and welcome to America."

By the time I returned to the bedroom, Evvie was in bed, turned on her side away from me. I hadn't unpacked my suitcase and couldn't even remember where it was. I just took off my dress, carefully put my shoes on the floor, and slipped into the bed.

It was a comfortable bed with a soft blanket that I pulled up to my neck even though it was a warm night. If Evvie knew that I was sleeping in my underwear, she would really despise me. How could I get her to like me? What could I say in my broken English that would make her see the kind of person I really was?

In France, even in the worst of times, I knew who I was, and I knew what to say. Mama sometimes complained that I had a big mouth and gave my opinions too freely. But here in America, I was speechless and lost.

I lay awake, thinking of the whole confusing day that had passed. As my ship sailed into New York Harbor earlier that morning, I stood on deck with other refugees from Europe, eagerly awaiting the first sight of the Statue of Liberty.

"There! There!"

Some of us wept, and others laughed. How magnificent she was, with her arm held up high, carrying the torch of freedom, and her beautiful head crowned with a splendid crown.

The Statue of Liberty was a symbol to us, coming from a past of pain and suffering, of a new land, a new beginning, where all good things were possible.

But lying there with Evvie's stinging words still loud in my ears, my unfamiliar family who understood nothing, the bewildering city that lay outside, I began to understand that America was more than just the Statue of Liberty.

CHAPTER 11

September 1947
Bronx, New York City

Y ou need to find a job," said my cousin Harriet. She and Evvie were eating breakfast in the kitchen. Evvie was studying something in a book and muttering. A plate of scrambled eggs and some toast lay untouched on the table before her.

"Put down that book and eat some breakfast, Evvie," said her mother, turning to look at her. "You haven't touched a bite. Now, eat something."

"I'm not hungry," Evvie grumbled. "And I need to study for my algebra test."

I had found my suitcase, selected a dark green, long-sleeved dress, washed up, combed my hair, and dressed. Evvie suddenly grinned.

I grinned back, surprised but pleased at this show of friendship. But she was not grinning at me. She was grinning at my dress. She didn't say anything to her mother but nodded in my direction. It was true that my dress was wrinkled, but it was one that my friend, Huguette, had passed on to me because it no longer fit her—a fine, dignified dress with a high neck and a slightly worn collar.

Now Harriet was smiling, too, so I knew something was wrong with the dress.

"Well, well," she said, "it's going to take time, that's for sure."

There was a huge platter of leftovers from the party in front of her.

"Anyway, Nicole—what a name!—what kind of food do you people eat for breakfast?"

"An egg," I said. "I like eggs."

I liked eggs very much, and even though more and more had begun appearing in France, I was still making up for being deprived during the war.

Harriet picked up a clump of food from her plate and put it into her mouth. She was a large woman, with a thick neck. I stood there watching how she chewed and waiting for her to offer me some breakfast.

Finally, after a few more mouthfuls, she said, "So go ahead and make yourself an egg! Don't think I'm going to wait on you hand and foot. There's eggs in the refrigerator, and the frying pan is on the stove."

I made myself an egg, found a plate and silverware, and joined them at the table.

"You don't have to be fussy," Harriet said.

"*Pardon?*" I asked.

"About a job. Just take what you can get. We can't support you. Don't expect that."

I ate my egg slowly. It was too delicious to gobble down, and so was the toast I learned to make, with real butter spread over it.

Afterward, I helped Harriet clean up the mess from last night's party. Many dishes had been stacked in the sink, but some still covered the dining room table. Napkins and silverware had been left on chairs and on the coffee table in the living room. Crumbs were scattered over the floor and on the sofa.

"Slobs!" muttered Harriet. "Some of them—Jake's cousin Harry and his family—your cousins, too—they have no manners. You'd think one of them at least could have stayed and helped clean up."

In between cleaning up and listening to Harriet's complaints, I had a chance to look around. The apartment had a sunken living room that opened into the dining room. All the furniture looked new. There was a big, fancy blue sofa, two matching blue-and-white-striped club chairs, a long coffee table, and two matching lamp tables with two matching blue lamps with matching white lampshades.

Just about everything in the apartment matched. Two pictures of flowers hung on the wall over the couch, and both looked almost the same. In both bedrooms, the furniture also matched.

Outside the living room window lay the Grand Concourse, a huge street with cars, buses, and yellow taxis speeding along. It was noisy, and also filled with hurrying pedestrians. It looked nothing like the streets of my town in France, which were quiet, with large trees lining them. People sat in outdoor cafes in my town, laughing and talking to one another.

I gathered up all the plates, glasses, and silverware, and I washed them. I swept the floor while my cousin Harriet sat in one of the club chairs, drinking her coffee and complaining that she was the one who was always stuck cleaning up at any party.

"All my life," said Harriet, "I've had to work hard, and who appreciates it? Your cousin Jake, I wait on him hand and foot and never get a thank-you. Here Nicole, here under the coffee table, you missed all those crumbs."

Evvie had left for school without saying good-bye to either her mother or me.

The kitchen was full of amazing things: a refrigerator with ice cubes in the top, a gleaming white stove, and something called a toaster, which I had discovered at breakfast. If you put a slice of bread into the top and pressed a knob, the bread descended, and after a few moments, toast popped up.

And so much soap! To wash your hands with. To put into the sink and create a mound of bubbles. All during the war, we had been unable to obtain real soap, and even now it was scarce in France.

I enjoyed washing the dishes. It felt luxurious using a double sink—one for soaping the dishes, and one for rinsing them. I held the silky bubbles in my hands and let them slide through my fingers.

The phone rang. Harriet, who had been napping, jumped up, answered it, and said, "Oh . . . yeah . . . oh . . . okay . . . here she is." She handed me the phone, and an excited voice said to me in French, *"Nicole, c'est moi."*

"Rosette," I cried, *"c'est vraiment toi?"*

It was wonderful to speak French again. I could be myself. With Harriet seated in the kitchen, though, I couldn't really answer all of her questions.

"My father will pick you up in his truck in about an hour and a half."

"A truck? Your father has a truck?"

"Oh, yes. He needs it for his work. So, plan on spending the week here, or more if you can. I have school, but I'll cut some of my classes. It's still warm enough to go swimming. I told your cousin—what's her name—Evelyn—that she should tell you to bring a bathing suit."

"She didn't tell me," I said.

"And my mother spoke to her mother. Didn't she tell you?"

"Just a moment." I turned to my cousin Harriet, whose face was squeezed into disapproving creases. Nobody wants to hear a conversation she can't understand, as I now knew perfectly well.

"My friend, Rosette Segal, and her family," I said, "they want me to be with them for a week. They said they (what was the English word for 'discuss'?) . . . they tell you—"

"Oh, that's right. I forgot," Harriet said, rolling her eyes. "I've been so busy getting things ready for you, I haven't had a minute. Anyway, that's fine. You go for a week and then you come back and find a job. Maybe they can help you."

"I can come," I said into the phone. "I'll be ready when your father comes. Oh, Rosette, it will be so wonderful to see you and your family!" I was close to tears.

Rosette laughed. "I'm not Rosette anymore. Now I'm Rose. And I can't wait to see you, too."

Harriet nodded when I hung up. "Well," she said, looking around the clean house, "you're quick. I'll say that for you. Maybe you could work as a cleaning woman."

CHAPTER 12

September 1947
Coney Island, New York

Rose's family had rented a small house for the summer in Coney Island, near the beach and boardwalk. Not only had Rose changed her name from Rosette to Rose, but she had also changed her appearance. I hadn't seen her in more than a year. When she left Aix-les-Bains, she was a skinny, short girl with a long, thin face and stringy hair. Now she had grown as tall as I, with a real figure and a rosy face. She wore an artificial flower in her short, curly hair, and she used makeup—lipstick, face powder, rouge, and even mascara.

She also looked at my green dress and shook her head.

"We need to go shopping," she said.

Suddenly, Rose had become the protector and I found myself the deferential follower.

Mme Segal went with us, and between them, they chose a sundress for me, a skirt, two blouses, a pair of shoes, a sweater, and a bathing suit. When I protested that they were spending too much, Mme Segal said, "Somebody has to buy you clothes. I don't think you can expect anything from that family of yours."

She couldn't stop talking about how hard she had to work before she could get my cousin Jake to bring me over to America.

"I visited him as soon as I received your letter with his address, and he said sure, he would fill out the papers when he had a chance. So, after a couple of months, I visited him again, and he said he just hadn't gotten around to it. But then, last October, he had a heart attack." Mme Segal smiled.

"I didn't know he had a heart attack," I said. "I'm sorry!"

"Sorry?" said Mme Segal. "Don't be sorry. It all worked out for the best. I visited him in the hospital a few times, and I told him over and over again that God would let him recover if he did his duty and brought you over. Then he promised—he swore—if he got better, he would bring you over. So, he recovered, and here you are."

I told them about Harriet and Evvie. I told them about all the cousins, and I told them that Harriet said I had to find a job right away, and that perhaps I should even consider becoming a cleaning woman.

Mme Segal muttered some strong words in French, and then sighed. "I suppose it never occurred to me that they would expect you to work. They have plenty of money, and I thought they would send you to school."

"It's fine," I reassured her. "I want to work. I don't want to take anything more from them. And as soon as I can, I will pay you back for all the clothes you bought me."

When we were by ourselves, I asked Rose what it meant to "get lost."

"It means that you should not bother somebody. It means you should go away from whoever is telling you that."

"It doesn't mean I need to lose myself in a forest?"

"There's no forest to get lost in anywhere in New York City," Rose laughed. "But now, I'll take you out to the boardwalk, and you be careful to stay with me, and not get lost."

DURING THAT WEEK with Rose, I was introduced to an amazing delicacy called a banana split. You cut a banana in half the long way, set it in an oval dish, pile any flavor of ice cream you wish over it, sprinkle it with nuts, drizzle chocolate syrup over the whole thing, and top it all with whipped cream and a maraschino cherry. I ate one every day.

"You will get fat," Rose warned.

Rose went to City College, but even when she was gone, I found pleasure in each new day. In the morning, I helped Mme Segal with her shopping, but afterward, she insisted that I go off and enjoy myself. I wandered the huge beach, lay in the sun, and swam in the salty ocean.

The beach was crowded with people, stretched out on blankets or sitting on deck chairs under colorful umbrellas. Mme Segal told me, "In the summer, you can hardly find any spaces you can squeeze into. It's impossible even to walk between all the people without stepping on somebody."

At night, Rose and I walked on the boardwalk and felt the ocean breeze on our faces. Rose looked for boys, and I looked for my banana split.

"There's David Bruckner over there. See, Nicole, he's pretending to look out at the ocean, but he really has a crush on me."

"Crush?"

"That means he likes me. He told his friend Larry, and Larry told my friend Dotty. He's nice-looking, isn't he?"

"Can I have my banana split now?"

"Oh, look, look, he's coming over. Let's act as if we don't see him."

ROSE'S ENGLISH SOUNDED perfect to me. She spoke without hesitation whenever an American said something to her, while I struggled to understand.

"You'll catch up," she assured me. "You were always one of the smartest in school."

I knew many of the words people used; I had studied them in school. But words and phrases like "crush," "get lost," "give me a break," or "what's the big deal?" left me lost and puzzled. I was particularly amazed by the expression "back and forth." Shouldn't it be the other way around? The formal English I had learned in school never covered idioms.

When I was alone with Rose and her family, we spoke French. As the week drew to a close, Mme Segal said to me one evening, "You know my husband is a carpenter. He works very hard, and many contractors like him. Luckily, he just recently was hired to do some work at the Waldorf-Astoria Hotel on Park Avenue in New York City."

"Is that the big, famous street in New York?"

"Yes, and many rich people live there. The Waldorf-Astoria is a hotel where other wealthy people stay."

"I would like to see it. I would like to see Park Avenue, and the Empire State Building, and all the important places in New York."

"Oh, you will," Rose said. "Maybe next weekend, I can take you and show you around. We can have lunch in the Automat and see a movie at Radio City and watch the Rockettes."

"I need to find a job," I told her.

"That's just what I was about to suggest," said Mme Segal. "Across the street from the Waldorf-Astoria, there is a store that sells only chocolate. According to my husband, there is a sign on the window that says 'Help Wanted.'"

I remained silent. "Help wanted" was one of those mysterious English expressions. I knew what "help" meant. You shouted "Help!" if you were ever caught in a fire or if somebody was robbing you. And I knew "wanted" meant

something you wished to have. But the two together—
"help wanted"—seemed totally meaningless.

"So, I thought," continued Mme Segal, "maybe you
would like to work there?"

"In a store that sells chocolates?" I cried. It sounded
like paradise. I had hardly eaten any chocolate during the
war and very little afterward.

"Why don't you stay until Monday? Meyer can take
you into the city, and bring you back to your cousin's
house in the Bronx. I will speak to your cousin's wife. I'm
sure she wouldn't object if it means a job for you. What
do you think?"

"Oh, yes, of course," I said. "But what does 'help
wanted' mean?"

CHAPTER 13

October 1947
New York City

Nobody else spoke French in *La Chocolaterie*. The owner, Mr. Ryan, hired me as soon as he understood that I spoke French. It didn't matter to him that my English was imperfect.

"We need somebody like you," he said. "It will give us a little more class." (What does "class" mean? I wondered. That was another word I would have to check with Rose.) "Just smile, speak a little French, and let somebody else handle the cash register."

He offered me thirty dollars a week and said I could start immediately. There were two older saleswomen, Rhoda and Lorraine. Each of us wore a pink-and-white-checked dress with a ruffled white apron. The whole store was painted pink, except for the display cases. Behind them was an amazing array of chocolates in little pink pleated papers. Customers could buy individual pieces of candy or boxes tied with a pink ribbon.

Rhoda, the younger of the two saleswomen, showed

me how to wrap the boxes in silver and white paper, and how to tie the ribbons.

"For a small box," she said, "use this thin ribbon, but for anything over a pound, you use this wide satin ribbon. Anything over five pounds, you tuck a sprig of these little dried pink and white flowers under the bow. Now, let's see you try it. That's not bad, but the bow should stand up. Try it again. That's better."

Rhoda was friendly, but not Lorraine.

"I never could understand," she told me, "why we had to fight in this war, anyway."

I tried to explain. "It was very bad," I told her. "Hitler killed a lot of people all over Europe—my own parents, too."

"But not here," she said, looking at me with distaste. "Why did we have to butt in? The war had nothing to do with us."

Millions of people had died in Europe, but Lorraine could not understand. Like most Americans, she had been sheltered from the horrors of the war. I kept away from her, or maybe she kept away from me.

Mr. Ryan, the owner, didn't seem to mind if his staff ate chocolates. He came in only to open the store and close it, collecting the proceeds of the day. Rhoda encouraged me to eat as many candies as I liked. She said she got sick of chocolates after a while, and thought she might even be allergic to them. Besides, she said, they weren't as good as Schrafft's.

I thought they were as good as any chocolates I had ever eaten in my whole life. Maybe I hadn't eaten enough to know the difference. The only problem for me was deciding among all the dazzling choices—nougats, nuts, marshmallows, creams, cherries, and coconut. There was also the problem of deciding whether I preferred milk chocolate or bittersweet.

I never could decide, which meant I had to keep trying.

At first, I felt shy with the customers, but after a while, I realized all I had to do was smile, say, *"Bonjour Madame* (or) *Monsieur, merci, au revoir."* Occasionally a customer spoke French, and then, while we conversed, other customers listened and smiled. From time to time, customers who spoke French as haltingly as I spoke English tried to speak to me, and I continued to smile, and slowly responded, never correcting what they said.

Many of the customers wore stylish clothes. The weather had turned cool, and some of the women wore fur stoles or fur coats. The theater season had begun, and we stayed open until nine, six days a week.

I never minded staying late, even the times I worked alone in the store. Without anyone there, I could eat as many chocolates as I liked. Often, I skipped dinner and gobbled down one chocolate after another. My English improved enough that I could understand orders and work the cash register. I learned that four quarters were worth one dollar; two dimes and a nickel were worth a quarter; five pennies, a nickel; and one five-dollar bill and two tens, twenty-five dollars.

Chocolates brought out the best in people. More customers in our store smiled than frowned. Eating chocolates made people happy, and bringing boxes of candy to somebody else made two people happy—the one who brought the box, and the one who received it. We saw more happy faces than unhappy ones in *La Chocolaterie*—except for Lorraine.

EVEN AT HOME, my cousin Harriet smiled. She asked me for twenty-five dollars of my wages, and I gave it to her.

"Of course, it doesn't really cover your food and board, and all your other expenses, but it's a start. And what kind of chocolates did you bring home today?"

At the end of every week, I filled a bag with assorted chocolates and brought them home to her.

"I really prefer milk chocolate," she said, biting into a bittersweet coconut cream candy, "but this one isn't bad. Here, Evvie, try a bite."

Evvie continued being sullen and aloof with me. I avoided her, and I no longer tried to please her. I visited Rose and her family almost every Sunday. They had returned to their small city apartment in Washington Heights, and Mme Segal now worked in a grocery store.

My cousin Jake, when he was around, was kind, and one day in late October, as the weather grew cooler, he said, "Nicole, come down to my shop. You can pick out a coat for yourself. It's too cold for you to keep wearing your sweater."

He said it when neither Harriet nor Evvie was in the room. Both of them now wore fur coats. Evvie's was a Mouton lamb, and Harriet's a Persian lamb. All up and down the Grand Concourse, women wore Persian lamb coats. It was almost a uniform.

Jake spoke to me in a low voice when neither Harriet nor Evvie was in the room. I had begun to understand that there might have been a reason why he was seldom at home, and judging from the loud arguments I sometimes heard from behind their bedroom door at night, I came to understand that this was not the happiest couple.

I took an extended lunch one afternoon and visited Jake's factory. It was a big one, with the sound of many sewing machines rattling away. Jake led me to a room with racks of coats. He showed me one with coats in navy blue, brown, and black.

"Here," he said. "These are nice and warm. Some of them even come with hats."

I didn't like any of the coats. They looked as if they were intended for old ladies, with their round collars and shapeless forms. My eyes wandered over to another rack of coats in bright colors—reds and blues and even some in pinks.

My cousin said, "Those are samples, expensive coats—our best line."

"Oh," I said, and tried to concentrate on the rack he had shown me.

A sudden wave of loneliness rose into my throat. I ran a hand down the old blue sweater my mother had picked for me. I thought about all the bright, pretty dresses and coats she had chosen for my sister and me. We were her children, and she loved us best in the world. Nobody would ever love me as much. I had to take a deep breath to keep from crying.

I didn't want one of those ugly coats. I shook my head, but kept my face down. I could hear my cousin sigh. "All right, Nicole," he said. "Go look at the samples. Go ahead."

I picked a red coat with a black velvet collar. It was a princess style, and it fit me perfectly. I looked at myself in the mirror and saw a dark-haired girl smiling back at herself. It was almost as if my mother had picked the coat out for me.

"Thank you! Thank you!" I cried. But it was not only for Jake. It was for my mother, too—for all the years I had never thanked her.

"It looks very nice, Nicole," he said, "and I hope you wear it in good health." Then he hesitated. "Maybe," he said, "maybe you should tell Harriet, when she asks you, that I gave you a discount on the coat and you plan on paying me back. Of course, you're not, but just tell her that you are."

"Oh, but I will, Cousin Jake," I told him. "*J'espère*, I hope, one *jour*, I mean day, to pay you and Cousin Harriet for everything you've done."

Jake sighed. "I don't want you to even think about it, Nicole. Harriet . . . well, Harriet . . . she isn't what I expected when we married. My daughter Sonia, you've only met her a couple of times. She's so much fun to be with! She's the way I thought Harriet was going to turn out, but . . . well, I was mistaken."

I mumbled about being grateful, and Jake continued. "I'm sorry she's such a . . . well, I'm sorry she is the way she is. It's not easy for me to be home with her. She complains all the time, and Evvie is growing more and more like her every day. I wish, I wish . . ."

He didn't say what he wished for. Suddenly, he checked his watch and said he had to meet with his buyer.

CHAPTER 14

January 1948
New York City

I must have gained ten pounds, and I had to move the buttons on my red coat so it would fit.

Mr. Ryan had some bad news for us at the beginning of January. "I'm going to have to close the store. Barton's opened a store a few blocks away, and Schrafft's is planning on opening one on Fifth Avenue. I'm losing too much money."

I felt guilty. I could feel my cheeks reddening. It must have been all those chocolates I had been eating that were responsible for poor Mr. Ryan's losing so much money.

"The three of you have been great workers," he said, "and I'll be happy to give you all letters of recommendation."

"Maybe," Lorraine said, looking sideways at me, "you have too many of us. Maybe you need only two people in the shop. Not three."

"No, no!" Mr. Ryan insisted. "When Nicole first came, I almost felt we'd make it—the customers liked her so much. But I just can't buck the competition." He raised his shoulders. "Who knows?" he said. "Maybe their chocolates are better than mine."

"Oh, no!" I shook my head. "Your chocolates are wonderful."

"Too bad others don't feel the same way," said Mr. Ryan.

He gave us a week's severance pay and let us take as much candy home as we liked.

THE CANDY KEPT Harriet in good spirits for a day or so. But it couldn't last forever.

"Now what are you going to do?" she asked.

"Do?"

"I mean work. You have to get a job. You can't just sit around eating candy."

I looked out the window at the snow falling, and said, "Mr. Ryan gave me a week's extra pay."

"Why don't you go over to Schrafft's or maybe a restaurant? They might hire you as a waitress. You might have to wash dishes for a while, but beggars can't be choosers."

Suddenly, Evvie piped up. "Well, Ma, you can't expect her to go out on a day like this. It's a real blizzard."

"So she'll take an umbrella and wear galoshes. I can't tell you how many terrible days I've had to go out to shop, to bring your father's shirts to the laundry—"

"Stay home, Nicole," Evvie said. And then, when I looked at her in surprise, she continued, talking angrily to her mother: "Why don't you just leave her alone for a change?" But Harriet simply continued to mutter about all the weather she had to brave, and how Jake never appreciated her.

YES, I WOULD HAVE TO get a job, and as soon as I could, I would move out. I watched Harriet's mouth enclosing a piece of caramel candy, and I realized how much I disliked her. Over and over again, Rose and her mother had invited me to come and stay with them. But they had a small apartment, and I didn't want to be a burden to them. In a few months, I would be eighteen. It was time, I decided, for me to be independent.

A FEW DAYS LATER, early in the morning, I took the train down to Rockefeller Center. Rose had suggested that I might find a job there. She had taken me down to Rockefeller Center during Christmas and had shown me the huge, magnificent Christmas tree with all its glittering ornaments. We looked down at the ice-skaters on the rink and watched as some of them spun and turned and danced on the ice. Neither of us knew how to ice-skate.

"One day," Rose said, "we'll learn to skate, and then the two of us will go skating."

I watched a man and woman twisting and spinning together on the ice. "I'm not sure," I said. "I don't think I could ever learn to look like some of them."

"Just look at that woman wearing the bright yellow costume with the black fur collar. If I ever learned to skate, that's what I'd like to wear."

"No, no," I insisted. "I like that red velvet one with the twirly skirt. And just look how she spins on one leg."

Suddenly, a girl standing next to us said shyly, "*Pardon. Je vous entends parler français. Vous êtes françaises?*"

Her name was Simone Leniger. Like us, she was also French and Jewish. She told us that, during the war, she had been separated from her family. Her parents had sent her to the south of France, where they believed she would be safer than in Paris. They kept her younger brother, who was still a baby, and managed to move to America. Finally, after six years, she had been reunited with them. But her parents and younger brother seemed uncomfortable with her. Sometimes they stopped talking when she entered the room.

Like me, she was struggling to learn English and to find herself in America. Often, she was so unhappy, she almost wished she were back in France, in the camp for displaced people where her friends seemed more like her real family.

She joined us when we had lunch at the Automat. I loved the Automat. There was nothing like it in France. I loved standing there with my nickels in my hand, surveying window after window, behind which plates of delicious foods lay. I could not remember ever seeing such an abundance of food in France, and for so little money.

Simone selected the fish cakes for fifteen cents. I chose the baked beans for ten cents. Rose splurged on the beef stew for twenty-five cents. For dessert, Rose selected the coconut cream pie, Simone the chocolate cake, and I the lemon meringue pie.

It was miraculous how, once you selected your food and put the required number of nickels into the slot, the window opened and you could pull out your food. Even more miraculous was how quickly a new plate with exactly the same food slid into the empty space, moved by unseen hands.

Soon Simone was smiling as we ate and talked about this strange country—America.

It turned out that Simone also lived in the Bronx, not far from me, and as we traveled home together, I realized that I had made a new friend.

BUT NOW, IN THE MIDDLE of January, on a freezing gray day, there was no Christmas tree sparkling in Rockefeller Center, no Automat, and no friends to support me. I stood there alone, leaning on the rail of the ice rink, looking down at the empty ice.

I found the personnel department at Rockefeller Center and rode the shiny escalator up to it. A smiling, well-dressed woman shook her head when I said I was looking for a job—any kind of job.

"We're letting people go," she said pleasantly, sitting in her warm office. "After Christmas, we always let people go. Come around next year—in late October or early November."

I took the shining escalator down and went out into the cold street. I hugged my red coat around me and stood helplessly under the gray sky. My fingers tingled with cold inside my gloves, and my teeth chattered. Where should I go next? I had to find a job. But where?

On Fifth Avenue, I passed St. Patrick's Cathedral and wondered if I should go inside to warm up and think. Just keep walking, I told myself. Something will come to you. And it did. I saw the sign just a block or two away. It said "Air France."

"No! No!" The young woman at the personnel desk shook her head and spoke to me in English. "We're not hiring anybody now. It's winter, and we don't have many flights. Besides, your English isn't very good. Why don't you go to school now, improve your English, and come back in the summer?"

"But I must find a job now, *Mademoiselle*," I insisted. "I am learning English, and I know I will be speaking better and better as the months pass."

"Well, I'm sorry, but we really don't have anything to offer you."

"I thought you might be able to use me because I speak French."

She shook her head impatiently. "Of course not," she said. "Almost everybody here speaks French, except for a few of us who deal with the public, and a few of the secretaries."

A handsome pilot came in, and she smiled up at him and said, "Why, Victor, it's been a long time. I was beginning to think you'd forgotten all about me."

He said something quickly, and she began giggling. But in between the giggles, she managed to motion with her head toward me. Dismissed!

MAYBE THAT WAS MY worst time in America, standing there in the warm room where two happy people flirted and laughed. I meant nothing to either one of them, and now I was about to go back outside, into the freezing gray day, with no place to go and only an unhappy home to took forward to, especially if I returned without a job.

The phone rang. Once . . . twice . . . three times, before the giggly receptionist could shake herself loose from the handsome pilot and answer the phone.

"Air France," she said.

Even from where I stood, near the exit, I could hear a very loud, angry voice coming through the phone.

"Oh," said the receptionist, losing her smile, "I didn't know."

The voice sounded even louder and angrier.

"But Mr. Dupuis, she never told me . . . yes, I understand . . . but . . . please . . . it's not my fault . . . I . . ."

She looked in my direction. "Just a moment, please . . . let me . . ." She covered the mouthpiece of the phone.

"Do you type?" she asked.

"Oh . . . yes," I lied.

"Mr. Dupuis, I have a young woman here who is looking for a job. She says she can type. Shall I send her up? She can come now . . . yes . . . right away . . . of course . . . immediately."

She hung up, and the pilot laughed. "Mr. Popularity, I take it."

"Shh!" she warned, and looked me over doubtfully. "One of our officers, Mr. Dupuis, needs some documents typed immediately. An assistant of his seems to have disappeared. Why don't you take the elevator up to the fifth floor, and ask for Mr. Dupuis."

"Sending lambs to the slaughter," the pilot murmured.

"Stop it!" she said to him, and pointed her finger in the direction of the elevator.

CHAPTER 15

r. Dupuis was waiting for me right outside the elevator. He looked like Hitler—a lock of dark hair on his forehead and a small moustache over his angry mouth. I felt tempted to turn right around and go back down in the elevator.

"What's your name?" he demanded.

"Nicole Nieman, *Monsieur*," I answered.

"Ah—*vous parlez Français?*" he asked in French.

"*Oui, Monsieur.*"

"Do you type?" he continued in French.

"Uh . . . yes."

"What kind of experience have you had?"

He fired one question after another at me, standing there in the hall—his anger increasing as he realized how little experience I had. "I can't understand how inefficient that personnel officer is. My assistant can't even speak French. And now, suddenly, she just doesn't show up. And she knew how much work I had for her today. Well, why are you standing there? You need to get started."

On the way to his assistant's office, M. Dupuis kept telling me about all the impossible secretarial assistants he'd had over the past year—all four of them. The first one was stupid. The second one was always taking sick leave. The third one just quit after only a week, and now the present one failed to show up today. He almost forgot about me while he angrily recited all his troubles with his secretarial assistants.

He led me into a small room with a typewriter on a desk, a chair, and a huge stack of papers.

"I needed copies of all of them today, but since you're off to a late start"—he looked at me as if it were my fault—"I suppose you'll need another day."

I looked at the top sheet. It dealt with parts of planes, and it was in English.

Suddenly, he began speaking English very quickly. It was difficult for me to understand. I stood there, stupidly looking at his moustache and the mouth moving below it. He stopped and said in English, "What's the problem? Don't you understand what I'm telling you?"

"Not completely, *Monsieur*. I just came over to America in September."

"That's wonderful!" he said angrily. "How can I get them to understand I need an assistant who speaks **both** English and French?"

"I speak French," I said proudly. "I finished my *Baccalaureat* before I left France, and my English improves continually."

He looked at me curiously. "Where did you come from?" he asked in French.

"From Aix-les-Bains, *Monsieur*."

"And your family? Did you all come over in September?"

"No, *Monsieur,* my parents and my sister were killed at Auschwitz. I came here by myself."

He looked away, and I continued, "I'm Jewish, *Monsieur.*" I waited for him to respond. If my religion made a difference to him, we needed to reach an understanding immediately. I would not work for anybody who was prejudiced against Jews. That was part of my past, and I determined, standing there, I would never allow it to be part of my future.

M. Dupuis turned to look at me. "I don't care what you are," he said, "as long as you can type up these papers."

I almost smiled. It was the kind of answer I had hoped for, even though I didn't know how to type.

"So hang up your coat and get started. I'll send in one of our typists to show you what the form should look like."

He left the room, and I looked around me. I felt like the girl in the fairy tale *Rumpelstiltskin,* trapped in a tiny place and ordered to turn straw into gold. I took off my coat, hung it on a rack, and examined the typewriter. I had never seen a typewriter before, and I certainly had never used one. I had no idea how to work it. I reached out and touched one of the keys. It said "s," and it yielded under the pressure of my finger. I saw a phone on the other side of the desk and reached for it.

I knew that Rose was still on school break between terms. Quickly, I dialed her number, and luckily, she answered it.

"Rose," I whispered, "do you know how to type?"

"Yes," she said. "I have to, because most of my teachers no longer accept handwritten papers."

"Well, tell me how to get started. I don't know how to type, and I won't get this job if I can't."

"Over the phone?" Rose asked. "You have to be kidding."

The door opened and a young woman entered, looking anxiously over her shoulder.

"I have to go, Rose," I whispered. "I'll call you later."

IT DIDN'T TAKE THE TYPIST long to figure out that I couldn't type. She was very kind and tried to show me how to put the paper into the typewriter.

"You see, you just slip it in here, and turn this knob. The only problem is that M. Dupuis wants two copies, so you will need to insert two carbon papers in between these three white papers. And if you make a mistake, you will need to correct all three papers individually."

I tried and tried. The papers never seemed to line up. "It takes patience and time," she said kindly. "And M. Dupuis is neither patient, nor does he have the time."

Finally, I managed to get all the papers lined up, and just as the typist was showing me how to hold my hands on the keys, the door opened and M. Dupuis entered the room.

"Well?" he demanded. "How many pages have you typed? You've been in here long enough."

The typist remained silent. I stood up and said, "I'm sorry to say, *Monsieur,* that I'm not really a very good typist—yet. I'm learning, and I hope that I will learn quickly."

"Are you telling me," M. Dupuis snapped, "that you are unable to type these pages for me?"

"Not at the moment, *Monsieur,* but I hope—"

"What do you hope?" he growled. "That next week, or next month or next year, you'll be able to type well enough to do this job that I need immediately?"

"I can try," I said.

He shook his head. "Why in the world," he asked, "did you tell them in personnel that you could type?"

I moved over to pick up my coat. "Because I needed a job and hoped it would work out, but I can see it won't."

"M. Dupuis," said the typist, "if you like, I would be willing to work overtime tonight. And I think that Leonora was planning to take tomorrow off as one of her vacation days, but perhaps she would be willing to take another day off instead and help out, too. I'm sure we could get the work done by tomorrow night."

He nodded and watched as I put on my coat.

"Just a moment," he said impatiently to me and picked up the phone. "Hello," he said, "Personnel? It looks like you did it again! I asked you to send me somebody who could type, because my assistant never showed up, and you send me an inexperienced girl who doesn't know how to type and who doesn't even speak good English, and . . . What? . . . She said she was going to take a test for her driver's license this morning, and she had told me yesterday? Well, I don't remember. Anyway, I don't want her anymore. She doesn't speak French, and she's not very intelligent. Find another place for her. I'll take this one. What's your name?" he asked in a cranky voice, turning to me. "Nicole Nieman," he reported back to personnel. "I like her spirit, and I think she'll fit in."

"Now," he told me as I stood there with my coat on, an astonished look on my face, "get your coat off and sit down at that desk. You're hired, and we'll pay you forty dollars a week to begin with. Once you've learned how to type, we can consider a raise."

He stormed out of the room and the typist said, "I can't believe it. M. Dupuis is the nastiest man in the whole world."

I hung up my coat quickly and sat down next to her. Maybe he would change his mind. I had to do something in a hurry to make him see I was going to try as hard as I could to repay him.

"Please," I said to her, "please, could you show me where I put my fingers on the typewriter keys?"

CHAPTER 16

March 1948
New York City

M Dupuis turned out to be very patient, at least with me. He was in charge of purchasing parts for Air France and shipping them overseas, as they were needed.

My job was to handle emergencies. If any parts for planes were desperately needed, I was expected to round them up. After the war, many planes had been dismantled, and it was my job to call or write companies like Lockheed that may have had surplus parts to sell. I was also expected to type any emergency documents that M. Dupuis required.

And I was finally learning to speak English.

"*Allo.*"

"What?"

"I mean, hello."

"Yes?"

"May I speak to the parts department?"

"This is the parts department. Who is this, please?"

"I am Nicole Nieman, an assistant to *Monsieur,* I mean, Mister, Dupuis of Air France."

A groan on the other end. "Okay, what does he want this time?"

"Well, *Madame,* I mean, Miss, we have a certain emergency and *il faut que* . . ."

"What?"

"*Pardon.* I mean we need two gas pumps, three rudder control switches, and ten altimeter gauges."

"And I suppose he wants them immediately, as usual?"

"Yes, Miss, yes. I know, Mister Dupuis, he is very—grateful. He says you are *très gentille*—I mean, very kind."

"Well, I do my best."

"We appreciate it very much."

"All right. I'll get them off to you. And what did you say your name was?"

"Nicole Nieman, Miss. It was really a pleasure speaking with you."

M. Dupuis was very pleased with my ability to find emergency parts. He was less pleased with my typing. I began staying late at work to learn how.

a-a-a-a

s-s-s-s

d-d-d-d

f-f-f-f

g-g-g-g

There was no reason to hurry home anyway. Although Cousin Harriet was impressed by my job and the twenty-seven dollars I now gave her, she was never kind. Evvie sometimes looked as if she wanted to say something to me, but most of the time she just kept her nose in her homework. I was beginning to wonder if she was shy.

One evening, M. Dupuis found me working on my typing at about seven-thirty. He sat down next to me and asked, "How is your typing going?"

"Much better, *Monsieur.* I still have trouble with the numbers and make too many mistakes on each page, but it improves."

"Good!" He nodded. "You know, Nicole, you are doing very well here. I like how you handle our emergencies. Some of the companies you have to deal with can be nasty."

"I'm used to nastiness," I said. "I can handle it."

"But you're young," he said. "You don't have to work overtime so many days. We don't pay you for that. Go home."

I made a face. "It's not comfortable at home. I live with my cousin and his family. My cousin is kind but hardly ever home. He and his wife fight a lot, and she's nasty to me. Her daughter, Evvie, she's my age. She's unhappy. I feel sorry for her, but we hardly ever have anything to say to each other."

What was the matter with me, babbling away like this to my boss? And even worse, suddenly I was crying.

"*Pardon! Pardon!*" I said behind my handkerchief.

M. Dupuis said softly in French, "Listen, Nicole, I know you haven't had it easy. But believe me, you have a lot going for you. Look how quickly you learned the job, and soon you'll be able to type as well as anybody else. You're smart, you're brave, and you'll have a happy future. I just know it."

Cranky, nasty M. Dupuis, speaking so gently now he reminded me of my father. His words made me cry even harder.

"Well, well," he said, patting my shoulder, "you can't help missing your family. They must have been wonderful people."

"Yes, they were," I sobbed.

"Tell me about them," he said.

And I told him. For the first time in America, somebody had asked me about my family. I told him how gentle my father was, how capable my mother, and how beautiful my little sister, Jacqueline.

To talk about them to somebody who listened intently was the greatest kindness for me, and to let me cry as I spoke showed what a good man he really was.

"My sister was only eight," I wept. "And I said mean things to her. I'll never be able to make it up to her."

"No," he agreed. "But you can make it up to yourself. That's what your family would want—living the life they should have lived. Even your little sister would have wanted that."

"She had a charm bracelet," I told him. "A little silver one that she loved. They ripped it off the night the Nazis took her and my parents. I wanted to give it back to her, but now I can't. Never! Never!"

I was still crying, and for a while, he said nothing. Then he stood up. "Nicole," he asked, "where is the little bracelet?"

"In my suitcase, I guess."

"Find it and wear it for her."

I nodded and wiped my eyes.

"Good," he said. "Now, how about friends? Do you have any friends?"

"Oh, yes, sir, two very good friends. And both of them are French."

"Well, go and have fun with them. You can work on your typing whenever you have time on the job. So, wash your face and go. And be here on time in the morning."

I WENT HOME and found Jacqueline's little charm bracelet. I slipped it onto my hand, and it fit. I jangled the little charms and thought about them. I could hear my mother's laugh and see Jacqueline's red curls as she bounced on my father's lap. I was crying again, but at the same time I felt a warmth inside me that had not been there for a long time.

CHAPTER 17

March 1948
New York City

Rose was in love. She often was in love, but this time, she told me, it was serious. His name was Alan Bernstein. "He's so smart, and he plans on being a physicist."

"He has no manners," her mother told me. "When he comes to take her out, he hardly says anything to my husband or me. He just mumbles."

"I keep telling you he's shy!" Rose yelled at her mother. "And you keep asking him one question after another. Why don't you say hello and leave him alone?"

Rose began to spend Saturday evenings with him, and sometimes Sundays. It meant I had to find other places to go on the weekends. Simone and I often got together because her home wasn't particularly inviting, either.

We began to talk more and more about moving out and finding a place together. Simone seemed to have problems with keeping a job, but she felt that, once we had agreed to move in together, she would have more incentive to keep one. The two of us began to explore the city. We liked the Forty-second Street Library, with the giant lions in front of it. Simone was enchanted with the Museum of Modern Art, and I loved the Museum of Natural History, with its big dinosaurs and precious jewels to look at. We began to feel more and more comfortable in the city.

ONE TUESDAY, Rose called me at work.

"Can you talk?"

"For a few minutes. I need to find a hydraulic pump and two control panel lights. So far, nobody I called had them."

"Well, listen, Alan has a friend named Jerry Soffer. He's very good-looking, and his sister gave him four tickets to the show *High Button Shoes*. So, let's double-date this Saturday."

"Double-date?"

"Oh, come on, Nicole—it means that the four of us go out together."

"But I don't know him."

"You are such a prude. I'll introduce you to him, and then you'll know him. They'll pick us up at seven-thirty at my house, but first, we'll go shopping."

"Shopping?"

"Yes, we'll have to get you some decent clothes and some makeup. I'll meet you about ten at Macy's. We can grab a bite at Chock Full o'Nuts, and then you'll come home with me and sleep over, so he won't have to take you home. He lives in Brooklyn."

"But, Rose, why do I have to buy new clothes? I have that black dress I bought when I got the job, and my brown skirt, and—"

"Trust me," Rose said. "You need a colorful dress— at least one. You look like a nun most of the time, except for your red coat."

"But, Rose—"

"Nicole, you're nearly eighteen and you've never gone out with a boy," Rose said. "And you need a bra."

"But why? I never wore one before. My slip covers me, and nobody ever said I needed one."

"Well, I'm telling you, you do. Every girl in America wears one, so let's go up to the lingerie department and we'll start there. I only hope we have enough time."

UPSTAIRS IN LINGERIE, a serious woman with a tape measure made me undress, and while I stood there, embarrassed, she discussed my dimensions with Rose.

"Thirty-two A. Do you want her to have a padded bra?"

"No!" I said.

"Yes," Rose said. "A little padding and a good pointed shape."

"I have just the one," said the saleswoman. "It's a good match with a girdle we have on sale now."

"Let's start with the bra. We'll probably need two or three."

I hated the feel of it. I hated the way it made me look when I put my sweater back on.

"I hate it," I told Rose. "It makes me stick out like a torpedo. I look like a freak."

"Hmm." Rose stepped back to look me over. "It's great. It makes you look like you really have something there. You don't want to look flat-chested, do you?"

"It's not comfortable."

"You'll get used to it." She turned to the saleswoman. "We'll take two in—what colors does it come in?"

"White, natural, and . . . maybe black."

"What color do you want?" Rose asked me. It was the only question she asked during our entire shopping expedition that day.

"Uh . . . white. But Rose, I don't really want it."

"Two in white," she told the saleswoman.

"And would you like her to try on the girdle?"

"No!" I insisted. "I won't wear a girdle. I won't!"

"All right," said Rose. "But you'll need something to hold up your stockings." She looked at my legs with their lisle stockings. "What's holding them up now?"

"Garters," I said. "I've always worn garters."

"Well, from now on, you're going to wear a garter belt, and you'll need some nylon stockings."

The garter belt proved to be an endurance test, which I failed. I kept twisting it around my waist and fumbling to attach my stockings to the little straps that hung down and ended in small buttons, which hooked onto the top of the stockings.

The nylon stockings with black lines down the back also proved impossible. The lines refused to run straight when I tried them on. They turned and twisted, no matter how I pulled at them.

"You'll learn," Rose continued to say, but more grimly each time.

She checked her watch. "We have time for a quick lunch."

"The Automat?" I asked hopefully.

"No, there's a Chock Full o'Nuts across the street. You can have a hot dog or a cream cheese–nut sandwich, and an orange drink."

"Do they have banana splits?"

"Nicole, we have some serious shopping to do, so let's get moving."

There were so many dresses on the racks in so many different colors, I was totally befuddled. Like everything else in America, there was always too much. I still found it hard to deal with more rather than less.

Rose moved easily between the racks. "Here," she said, picking up a dress with a scoop neckline and a flared skirt. "It's pretty, don't you think?"

It was pretty, with stripes of many colors. But when I tried it on, I told Rose that the neckline was too low.

"The neckline is fine. Do you have a pretty necklace?"

"I have pearls at home, but nothing with me."

"I'll lend you something for tonight." Rose looked at her watch. "Now we'd better get you a pair of shoes. You need a lot of other things, but we're running out of time."

"What's the matter with the shoes I'm wearing?"

Rose looked down at my sensible, flat-heeled brown shoes.

"Nothing's the matter with them. They're fine for work, but they're not dressy enough. Now let's find out where the shoe department is."

Rose selected a pair of black pumps with a Cuban heel—about two inches from the ground.

"They're not comfortable," I complained. "I can hardly walk."

"You're not supposed to walk in shoes like that. And you won't have to walk. We'll only get on the train and off the train when we go to the theater. Maybe we'll have a bite afterward, so you'll be sitting most of the time. The heels on my pumps are even higher. Nobody wears flat shoes to go out on a date."

Rose had hoped to spend some time in the cosmetics department, where a saleswoman could show me how to wear makeup properly. But time was running out and so was my money.

"I'll fix you up at home. We can skip dinner, and then I'll have time to work on you. There won't be time to tweeze your eyebrows, but they aren't too bad. Mine are really bushy."

Mme Segal insisted that we eat something, so we gulped down our food and then Rose sat me down in front of the vanity in her bedroom and went to work. She powdered my face and put a touch of rouge on my cheeks. Then she had me close my eyes, and she brushed some blue color on my eyelids and black mascara on my eyelashes.

"Good thing your complexion is good," she said. "Otherwise we'd have to use pancake makeup."

She put bright lipstick on my mouth and then began combing my hair.

"Too long," she said. "If you'd set it with curlers, you could wear it in an upsweep."

"Upsweep?"

"You know, with curls on top of your head. But—I wish I had thought of it before—you need to go to the beauty parlor and get a feather cut—remember, a feather cut. It's a short cut, in layers. Anyway, you do have a little curl, so we'll just let it hang straight with a front part. There. After you're dressed, I'll comb it over again and lend you an artificial flower to wear on one side of your head. Maybe this pink one. Now, hurry, get dressed. I still have to make myself up. They'll be here at seven-thirty, and it's seven o'clock now."

I tried to hurry, but the garter belt kept twisting and ended up sideways. Rose had to help me, and she also had to straighten out the seams on my stockings.

Finally, at twenty after seven, I was dressed, and Rose pinned a pink flower in my hair.

She stepped back and smiled. "Now," she said, pulling me over to a full-length mirror, "what do you think?"

A stranger looked back at me from the mirror. She had a face covered with makeup, stood on legs that wobbled in shaky shoes, and wore a dress that revealed more of her chest than seemed decent.

"Rose," I said, "I don't look like me."

"You look wonderful," she said, patting the pink flower in my hair. "Just keep adjusting the flower with bobby pins so it doesn't fall off your head."

"But I don't want to look like this," I said. "I want to look like me."

And that's when the doorbell rang.

CHAPTER 18

The Same Evening

Rose walked into the room, an arm around each boy's shoulder.

"Nicole, this is Alan," she said, patting the shoulder of the boy on her left, her boyfriend. "And this"—she continued, patting the other boy's shoulder—"is Jerry."

Jerry, my date, smiled and said, "Howreyou?" He detached himself from Rose and held out his hand to me. "Hello," I said nervously, shaking his hand. He sat down next to me and began talking about how lucky he was to get the four tickets to *High Button Shoes*.

"My sister's husband got sick, and the couple they were going with forgot the date and had to go to a bar mitzvah. My sister gave me the tickets and didn't even ask me to pay for them. She's so angry at her friends she says she's going to make them pay."

Rose giggled. "Oh, I've been dying to see it," she said. "I hardly ever go to a Broadway show. My aunt took me to see *Oklahoma*. I just loved it."

"I never go to musicals," Alan said. "They're silly. I'd rather see a foreign movie like *Open City*."

"You're just a snob." Jerry shook his head. "Nicole, what do you like?" he asked, turning toward me.

"Oh, me . . . well . . ." What did I like? "I've never seen a Broadway show," I admitted. "But I do go to the movies. Sometimes, they speak English so fast, it's hard for me to understand everything."

I thought about the Loew's Paradise Theater on Grand Concourse. It was such a beautiful theater, it hardly mattered which movie I saw. Up on the domed ceiling, stars seemed to twinkle, and the whole theater, with its gilded furnishings, looked so splendid, it made me feel as if I were a rich aristocrat. Sometimes Simone and I went, when she could afford it.

"There are plenty of fine French movies," Alan said. "Have you ever seen any of Jean Cocteau's, for instance?"

"Oh, yes," I said. "In France, I saw *La Belle et La Bête.*"

"What did you think of it?"

"I thought it was beautiful. I wish I could see more French movies."

Rose's parents came into the room, and Rose stiffened. She focused a meaningful look in her mother's direction, but both of them behaved.

"Good evening!" said M. Segal. Jerry stood up and shook hands with him.

"Good evening to you, sir, and you, too, ma'am," he said, shaking hands with Mme Segal. Alan mumbled something but stayed at Rose's side.

"Is it cold out?" Rose's mother asked.

"Yes, it is for March," Jerry answered, as if it were a serious question.

I could see that Mme Segal approved of Jerry, but not of Alan. She barely glanced at him. Jerry spoke easily to both of Rose's parents, while I inspected him. Middle height, well built, good-looking, with dark, curly hair and very comfortable manners. I liked him and began looking forward to the evening.

Jerry held my elbow whenever we crossed a street, while I wobbled along in my new shoes. In the theater, he helped me off with my coat.

During the intermission, Jerry and Rose did most of the talking.

"It's so clever," Rose said, "and the music is wonderful."

"I don't think so," Alan grumbled.

"The dancing is great, too," Jerry said. "I really laughed my head off at that crazy ballet."

"Did you notice how one of the dancers kept falling all over the place?" Rose laughed. "But maybe she's supposed to. It's such a kick."

"I think so, too," Jerry agreed.

"Anyway, will you excuse us for a few minutes?" Rose said, taking me by the hand. "We need to freshen up."

"So?" Rose asked when we were in the ladies' room. "What do you think of Jerry?"

She powdered her nose in front of the mirror, and she powdered mine, too.

"Stop!" I said. "He's nice, but doesn't your boyfriend ever talk?"

"He's serious," Rose said. "He likes to talk about serious things like politics or Shakespeare. We always go to foreign movies when we go out, or to the Davenport Free Theater, or to Lewissohn Stadium for cheap concerts. He doesn't have much money, and I'm certainly not going to pay my own way."

"Why not?" I asked.

"Because it's not right for a girl to pay. Anyway, put on some more lipstick, and then let's go join the fellows."

After the show, we went to Toffenetti's restaurant. They are famous for their strawberry shortcake, Jerry said.

"But it's early for strawberries."

"Yes, but they probably freeze them and bury them under lots of whipped cream. Go ahead. Try it. I guarantee you'll like it."

I tried it, and I did like it. Jerry and Rose also ordered the strawberry shortcake, but Alan had only a cup of coffee and a plain doughnut.

Rose and Jerry talked on and on about *High Button Shoes*. Alan and I were silent.

LATER, BACK HOME, Rose's mother was waiting up for us. "Did you have a good time?" she asked.

"Yes, we did," Rose answered disdainfully.

Rose's attitude toward her mother always astonished

me and made me jealous. The way I saw it, of course Rose's mother would be interested in her daughter, the way my mother had been interested in me and my sister. My mother would have wanted to know what kind of evening I had spent. I'm sure I wouldn't have answered her the way Rose answered her mother.

I said, "We had a very nice evening, Mme Segal. The play was very good, and after, we went to Toffenetti's, and three of us had strawberry shortcake."

"Did Alan have strawberry shortcake?"

"Ma! What difference does that make? Stop being so nosy."

"He had coffee and a doughnut, *Madame*."

"Of course."

"Now what's that supposed to mean?" Rose yelled.

While Rose and her mother shouted at each other, I stood there, missing my mother so much, I had to run out of the room and cry in the bathroom.

"He's a nothing!" I heard Mme Segal yell. "You always pick rude, unpleasant boys. Why can't you pick a nice, friendly boy like that other one?"

I remembered how Rose had clung to her mother in France after they were reunited. I also remembered some of the times I had argued with my mother, and the many times she had said I had a big mouth. But I could not believe that, had my mother returned, I would ever have treated her the way Rose was treating her mother.

When I looked at myself in the mirror, the mascara had mixed with my tears, and streaks of it ran down my cheeks. I washed my face; cleaned off the mascara, the powder, the rouge, and the eye shadow so that I looked like me again. I looked the way my mother would have approved.

LATER, IN ROSE'S bedroom, she and I talked in low voices about the boys.

"It's a funny thing," Rose said. "Usually, if my mother likes a boy, I don't. But that Jerry—he's pretty cute."

"I guess he is."

"Do you . . . are you interested in him?"

"I don't know. But I don't think he's interested in me. He hardly said anything to me all evening."

Rose appeared thoughtful.

"Do you like him, Rose? Would you like to go out with him?"

"Well, I'm thinking of breaking up with Alan. I really thought of it before tonight. He's so serious. I'm getting sick of foreign movies and Lewissohn Stadium. But if you . . . I mean . . . if you like Jerry . . ."

"He's nice, but I could see he liked you, Rose, so if you want to go out with him, don't worry about me."

"Are you sure?"

"I'm sure."

CHAPTER 19

April 1948
Bronx, New York City

Happy Birthday!" said Simone. She insisted on treating me to a banana split at Krum's on the Grand Concourse.

"But you have no money," I protested.

"I will, by the end of next week. If you lend me some, I'll pay you back then."

She sipped her chocolate soda and daintily dug out scoops of vanilla ice cream with her long spoon.

The teenage boy who handled the counter kept wiping off the space next to her and asking if she needed more water.

"No, thank you," she said, smiling graciously. "Did you see his pimples?" she asked me, after he had moved away. "It's disgusting."

Simone always attracted attention because of her lovely face. Her hair was dark, almost black, and her eyes a deep blue against her soft, pale skin. Unlike Rose, Simone hardly ever dated, but she enjoyed the attention.

"How did you get the job?" I asked, as soon as I could raise my eyes from the banana split. Krum's really understood banana splits, and I had become an expert.

"Oh. I took my brother to the dentist—Dr. Lyons— and he asked me if I wanted a job as a receptionist."

"Just like that?"

"Well, I did act very sweet to André—the nasty brat—and did show a lot of admiration for Dr. Lyons's skill." Simone grinned. Her teeth were white and straight. "He commented on how fine my teeth looked, and I said . . . well, one thing led to another, and he offered me the job. I'm not sure his hygienist was pleased."

"If you keep it, Simone, we can each move out and find a place together."

Simone sighed. "I hope so, but . . . well . . . I'm different from you, Nicole. You're sort of a worker bee, and I don't know how to be one."

"I had no choice," I said.

Simone shook her head. "Even in France," she said, "somebody always took care of me in the camp, and here—well, my parents may not be happy with me, but they never expect anything, either. They'd be happy if I left. I just don't know how to work hard. But I'll try."

Simone carefully scraped around the bottom of her glass. "Oh, here he comes again."

The young man cleaning the counter was back again, wiping away.

I lingered over my banana split. There was only a small piece of banana left and some half-melted coffee ice cream.

Simone ignored him. "Now," she said, "it's your birthday. Where should we go?"

"Well, I could use another dress. I haven't bought anything for when the weather warms up. And maybe a sweater for now. Could we go to Alexander's? It's only a few blocks away."

By now, I could wear my pumps with the Cuban heels. Not every day, but since today was my birthday, I thought I should dress up. I was wearing my black dress with pearls. I had learned how to handle the garter belt, and the seams of my nylon stockings ran straight down my legs.

I didn't feel as intimidated as I used to by all the well-dressed American women who surrounded me on the subway, the streets, and even here in Krum's. More and more, I wanted to look like one of them.

"See that girl over there with the blond hair?" I whispered to Simone. "She's wearing a matching sweater set. Doesn't she look pretty?"

Simone shrugged. She wasn't much interested in fashion. With her beautiful face, it hardly mattered what she wore.

"Look how she's laughing with the boy. Maybe he's her boyfriend. He looks good in his leather jacket, doesn't he?"

"Americans laugh too much," Simone said. "They didn't really suffer the way we did during the war. They're like children."

"It's true," I agreed. "But it's not their fault. They can't understand. Some of them try, but it's always been so easy for them. I try, too. I want to forget, but sometimes . . . sometimes . . . it's hard."

Simone took my hand and pressed it. "Don't you ever want to go back to France? At least people there understand."

"No! No!" I almost cried. "I don't want to go back. It's too sad there. I want to stay here. I need to forget and move on. I have to."

"There was a boy there," Simone said, almost dreamily. "He was older than the rest of us, and he helped take care of us. He was so good, so kind . . . he said he would write to me. I guess he thought I was a kid . . . but he promised, and he never did."

"Simone," I asked, "did you like him?"

She nodded, and then she shook her head. "But I have to forget about him, too, and move on."

"Why don't you write to him?"

"I don't know where he is. Anyway, let's go to Alexander's. I don't mind poking around there, even if I don't have any money."

"I can lend you some," I offered, as we walked toward Alexander's, the big department store on Fordham Road.

"That's okay," Simone said. "I'm not going to need more clothes for my job. I'll be wearing a white coat over everything. Anyway, is your family doing anything for your birthday? Did they give you that bracelet?"

"No. They don't even know it's my birthday," I told her.

"I guess you're worse off than I am, in a way," Simone said as we entered the store. "My family at least tries to act as if they care for me. Yours doesn't even try."

I bought a new dress: a short-sleeved, blue-flowered one with a collar and covered buttons down the front. It was even prettier than the striped one with the scoop neck Rose had picked out for me, and a lot more comfortable to wear. I only wished I had someplace to wear it.

"I'm going to have to run," Simone said. "It's my parents' anniversary, and they expect me to help celebrate. Are you going someplace tonight?"

"No. Harriet and Evvie are going to the movies. Evvie sort of invited me, but I could see that Harriet wasn't happy, so I politely declined."

"Well, why don't you come to my house? I'm sure my parents wouldn't mind," Simone said.

I thought of Simone's small apartment and her awkward parents. I doubted that they wanted me to come, and I could see she wasn't sure either.

"Thank you, but I want to shop a little longer."

"How about Rose?" Simone asked. "Could you get together with her?"

"Rose has a date tonight with her new boyfriend, Jerry."

"Well, come home with me then."

"No, I really want to do a little more shopping."

Simone seemed relieved. "If that's what you want,

okay, but in another few weeks, we'll start looking around for an apartment. It's unbearable for both of us."

She kissed me and wished me a happy birthday. After she left, I bought a pale pink sweater set and felt exhilarated when I looked at myself in the mirror. I had cut my hair in a feather cut, and to everybody just looking at me, I was a happy American girl—on the outside. I fingered the charm bracelet. On the inside, it was different.

CHAPTER 20

April 1948
Bronx, New York City

There was a call for you," said my cousin Harriet. "Who was it?" I asked. I had just returned from work, and I could smell dinner. I had to admit that Harriet was a good cook, and she never resented my interest in food as long as I cleaned up afterward and did all the dishes.

"I don't know. I could hardly understand him—he mumbled so. He's probably French, but he said he would call back later."

Conversation at dinner concerned my cousin Jake. "I told him tonight to try to get home for dinner, but he said he had a meeting. It's always something with him. He's like a boarder in this house."

Evvie suddenly said to me, "That's a new sweater set, isn't it?"

"Yes, I just bought it last week."

"Where did you get it?"

"At Alexander's."

"See!" she said to her mother. "That's the kind of set I want."

"So, go shopping," her mother said. "Maybe you can get it in a nicer color. Maybe in blue. You look good in blue."

"And what's that you're wearing?" Evvie asked. "Is it a charm bracelet?"

"Yes." I held out my arm so she could see it. "My little sister, Jacqueline. It belonged to her."

"Oh, I didn't know you had a sister." Evvie looked as if she wanted to say something else, but the phone rang, and she jumped up to answer it. "Oh," she said, ". . . yes, she is . . . hold on." She handed me the phone.

"*Allo!*" I said. It was still hard for me to say "hello."

"Uh . . . hello . . . Nicole?"

"Yes, who is this, please?"

"It's Alan Bernstein. Remember . . . I used to go out with Rose."

"Of course, I remember."

"Well . . . I just wondered . . . there's a movie theater showing Jean Renoir's film *Rules of the Game*. Let's see, in French, it's called *La Regle Du Jeu*. I'm sorry, I know I'm not saying it right. I took Spanish in school. But I wondered if you would like . . . well, to go with me to see it?"

There was a nervous pause on his end of the phone.

"Yes," I said, "I would like to go. I would love to see a French movie."

"It has English subtitles," he warned.

"I don't have to read them," I said.

"Are you free on Saturday?"

"Yes, I am."

"It's playing at eight, so I'd better pick you up at about seven."

"Yes, that's good. Thank you. I'll be ready."

We spoke a little longer about where I lived, and then I hung up.

Evvie asked, "Are you going out with a boy?"

"Yes, I met him at my friend Rose's."

"A Jewish boy?" Cousin Harriet asked severely.

"I think so. His name is Alan Bernstein," I answered. I stood up and began carrying the dishes into the kitchen.

Later, Evvie said to me, "You shouldn't say thank you."

"To whom?"

"To the boy who's asking you for a date. You're not supposed to thank him. You're doing him a favor by going out with him."

"Oh!" I said. "But he's taking me to the movies. So why shouldn't I thank him?"

"Forget it!" Evvie said. "Just forget it."

I was about to ask her when were you supposed to say thank you to a boy who was taking you out, paying your way, picking you up, and taking you home. I was about to ask her what she does on a date, but then I remembered that Evvie didn't date. Ever since I had come to stay with them, I had never seen Evvie go out with a boy.

She was unhappy, I knew that. She was unhappy about how she looked, her inability to have friends, her family. I thought about myself. If I was unhappy now, it was not because of who I was or the kind of family I'd had.

"Thank you, Evvie," I said.

"For what?" she asked.

"For telling me how to behave with American boys. I didn't know."

"Well, I was only trying to help," she said, almost smiling.

I CALLED ROSE to make sure she didn't mind.

"Why should I mind?" Rose asked. "I was glad to get rid of him. But you don't have to go out with him just because he asks. He's too serious."

"Well, I'm serious, too—and he's taking me to a French movie."

Rose giggled. "Maybe we can double-date one night. Only you have to promise not to switch partners."

"I wanted you to tell me what to wear, Rose."

"It doesn't matter what you wear, Nicole. Alan doesn't notice what anybody wears."

NEVERTHELESS, THE REST of the week, I worried about my clothes. When nobody was home, I tried on different outfits—my black dress, my new one, the sweater set, a white blouse with a scarf, without a scarf, and variations on all of the above.

When seven o'clock came, I was seated on the couch, dressed in my sweater set, with the pearl necklace, my gray skirt, my charm bracelet, and my black pumps and nylon stockings.

"No, no," said Evvie. "Go into the bedroom. You're not supposed to be ready. My mother will answer the bell. Go!" She came with me and sat next to me on my bed, waiting.

The doorbell rang, and I heard Cousin Harriet's loud voice greeting Alan. I could hardly hear his.

"Just wait!" Evvie whispered.

After about five minutes, she nodded, and both of us entered the living room. Alan was crammed into a corner of the sofa while Cousin Harriet chatted away at him.

"Ah, here she is," Harriet said, smiling at me as if she really cared about me.

Maybe I would have felt shy ordinarily, but seeing Alan's discomfort made me brave.

"Hello, Alan," I said. "This is my cousin Evvie. I see you've met my cousin Harriet."

Alan mumbled something, and Evvie smiled and asked him if he knew her friend's brother, Ernie Heller, who also went to City College.

Alan said he didn't.

"Is it cold outside?" asked Harriet.

Alan said he hadn't noticed and looked helplessly at me.

"Well, I guess we'd better go if we don't want to miss that movie," I said.

"Now, don't keep her out too late," said Harriet sweetly. "And have a good time."

When we were outside, Alan said gloomily, "She's very friendly, isn't she?"

"No," I said. "She's not friendly at all. But you seem to bring out the best in her."

"Something must be wrong with her," Alan said.

CHAPTER 21

April 1948
New York City

All the way to the subway station, Alan kept complaining about the unrealistic movies Hollywood produced.

"Only the foreign films deal with the real world. Mostly I see Italian or French movies, and sometimes an English one from England. Who wants to see Ginger Rogers and Fred Astaire act like all you have to do is tap-dance to live a happy life?"

I smiled but didn't respond. I loved Ginger Rogers and Fred Astaire but was afraid to admit it.

"Once in a while," Alan said as he followed me down the stairs to the subway, "you get somebody like Charlie Chaplin, who understands irony. Did you see *The Great Dictator*?"

Before I had a chance to answer, he yelled, "Oh, look, the train's coming. Hurry! Hurry! I'll hold the door open. Hurry!"

He dashed ahead of me, put some nickels in the slot, rushed through the turnstile, into the train, and held the door, while I stood staring at him on the other side of the platform.

"Oh, no!" Alan let go of the train door and shook his head. "I goofed again," he said. "I can't do anything right."

Both of us watched as the train moved out of the station. Then Alan examined the coins in his pocket as we stood on opposite sides of the turnstile.

"I guess I don't have enough nickels, either."

"That's okay," I told him, examining the change in my purse. "I have a few."

I put my nickels into the slot and joined him on the platform.

"I can give you back the change," he offered awkwardly. "I have a couple of dimes and a quarter."

"Don't worry about it," I told him.

"Most girls expect the boy to pay for everything, so if you feel the same way—"

"I'm not so fussy," I told him.

Alan checked his watch. "We'll have plenty of time. But I just wasn't thinking."

"It's not important."

"Well, yes, it is. I do a lot of dumb things. Especially with girls."

"Forget it!"

But he couldn't. All the way to the movie theater, he kept telling me about how clumsy he was, how awkward, and how sorry he always was afterward.

"You should be yourself whoever you are with—boys or girls," I lectured. "It's always a mistake to try to be somebody you aren't. Girls are going to be just as uncomfortable around boys."

Alan seemed very young to me—not the way a nineteen-year-old was supposed to be. Certainly not the way Jerry had behaved. I tried to change the subject, and by the time we reached the theater, he had stopped apologizing.

We had about twenty minutes to wait before the movie started. A number of casually dressed young people stood in the lobby, talking and laughing. Some of them knew Alan and said hi.

One of them hurried over. "Alan, Alan!" he cried. "I missed physics class yesterday. Can I have a look at your notes?"

"Sure," Alan told him. "You missed a good one. Professor Leland lectured on Einstein's unified field theory. He really knows his stuff."

Alan and his friend continued discussing Einstein's unified field theory, using words I couldn't even begin to understand. He forgot to introduce me to his friend, and to another boy who joined them in the conversation. I stood awkwardly to one side while they spoke very animatedly about matters that had nothing to do with my real world.

A young woman approached me.

"Excuse me," she said. "Are you here with Alan Bernstein?"

"Yes, I am."

"Well, I'm here with Jeff."

"Jeff?"

"He's the one who's going on and on about Einstein. My name is Norma Jackson. What's yours?"

"Nicole Nieman. I'm glad to meet you."

"You're probably glad to meet anybody. Come over here, away from all their yatting. Alan's very smart. He's probably going to win the Nobel Prize one day, but there aren't many girls who are willing to put up with him. And most girls here in America put up with a lot. You must be that friend of Rose's Alan's been talking about."

"Yes, Rose is my friend. But what's he been saying?"

Norma looked me over. "Well, he told Jeff you were very pretty and very interested in foreign movies."

Alan had said I was very pretty! It made the whole evening worthwhile. Even though he was awkward, child-like, boring, and not good-looking, I began to think he might have some compensating qualities.

"Let's get some popcorn," she suggested.

"Popcorn?"

She began pushing her way over to the candy counter, and I followed. She bought a huge cardboard box with something yellow inside.

"Here, have some," she said, holding out the box.

Carefully, I picked up a small piece and put it into my mouth. It tasted like nothing I had ever eaten before—not exactly soft, not exactly hard, not dry, but not wet, either.

"Oh, take some more," she urged, shoving a handful into her mouth.

"I have never tried it before," I said, chewing slowly.

"Oh, don't they have it in France?"

I shook my head, then picked up a few more pieces and chewed a little faster. "It has butter and salt?" I asked.

"Yes, plenty of both."

"What's it made of?"

"Dried corn. They pop it."

"Pop it?"

Norma smiled indulgently. "Just take a little more. I think you'll like it."

She was right. I liked it a lot, even though I didn't understand what it meant to pop dried corn.

By the time Alan ran over to me, apologizing and blaming himself for ignoring me, I just said, "Let's buy popcorn."

All during the movie, we ate popcorn. As far as I was concerned, it was the best part of the movie. Afterward, as Alan went on and on about the artistry and irony of the movie, I silently disagreed with most of what he was saying.

The movie dealt with a group of rich French people before the war started, who were so busy with their own selfish concerns that they could not see what was going to happen to them. I didn't know any rich French people who hunted and lived in country mansions and had affairs with the wives of their married friends. The muddled English titles mixed me up as I tried to listen to the French, and I kept losing the thread of the story. But none of the characters seemed at all likable.

In my real world, the people I knew who had suffered in the war were neither rich nor lived in country mansions. But I smiled and nodded at whatever Alan said, and tried to act like a real American girl.

CHAPTER 22

June 1948
New York City

There was so much I had to understand about fitting in. As my English improved, I learned how important it was to say no. In France, the word *no* had never posed a problem for me. My mother often complained that I used it too often. But in America, intimidated as I was by so many things, it took me nearly a year to become brave enough to say no.

Most of my fellow workers smoked, and the air outside my office was foul. I mentioned it one day to Anne-Marie Barrault, one of the other assistants to M. Dupuis.

"You need to learn," she said firmly. "It makes you look sophisticated. People respect you more if you smoke. Otherwise, you look uninteresting. Just watch the movies—Humphrey Bogart smokes, Lauren Bacall smokes, and all the famous artists, like Picasso—at least, I think he smokes."

"Not me," I said. "It smells bad."

Anne-Marie grinned. "Oh, I'm not letting you off the hook. We have to make a real American girl out of you."

One night, she gathered three other girls: Louise Delon, Helene Sardou, and Michelle Benoit. They invited me to join them for dinner at the New York Cafeteria, an invitation I was happy to accept. Cafeterias, next to the Automat, were my favorite places to eat. Just standing in front of a steaming counter heaped with an assortment of dishes, from hot turkey sandwiches to rice pudding, and inhaling the aromas of so much fragrant food seemed unbelievable.

As ever, we enjoyed our food, our gossip, and our shared admiration of the handsome pilots.

Michelle cleared the table and signaled for me to stay where I was.

"Just sit there," she ordered. "We have a plan in mind for you."

The others smiled, as Anne-Marie Barrault fished around in her purse.

"What's happening?" I wanted to know.

"We want to teach you to smoke," she explained.

"But I never said I wanted to learn."

She passed the pack around to all the other girls. Each selected a cigarette and lit up.

"Now!" Anne-Marie offered me one. "Take a cigarette and try it. Just try it. That's all we want."

I watched them as they inhaled, and surprisingly, it did look good. I had to admit there seemed to be a camaraderie among smokers, and Louise, a willowy blonde with a bright red mouth, did look glamorous as she blew out a straight line of smoke.

"All right," I said, "I'll try." I took a cigarette, and Anne-Marie said, "Before I light it, just watch me. See, you pull in your breath with the smoke, like this." She inhaled and held the smoke in her mouth, shaped her lips into an O, and released the smoke in the shape of a series of circles."

"That looks hard to do," I said.

"Well, right now, just learn to inhale. Breathe the smoke in, and let it out as slowly as you can. Later, you'll learn how to make lots of different shapes."

I put a cigarette into my mouth, and Anne-Marie lit it with a silver lighter.

"Now, breathe in," she instructed.

I breathed in.

"Now, out."

I thought I would choke, and began gagging and coughing right in Anne-Marie's face.

"That's okay," she said kindly. "It's always hard the first time. Take a few minutes, and then try again."

"It's terrible," I protested. "I hate it."

"Most of us do in the beginning, but we get used to it."

"No!" I shook my head. "No, I won't."

"We'll try again, another time," Anne-Marie said. "You'll come around."

"No!" I said.

• • •

DATING GAVE YOU a certain status, and I enjoyed being part of a successful group of girls who had boyfriends. But after three or four evenings of listening to Alan's complaints about his own inadequacies, and everybody else's, I had had enough.

I didn't have to ask Rose or Simone. I just knew that the correct answer was no.

"But why?" Alan asked.

"Because I don't think we're really the same type. I mean, you're very smart, everybody says that, but you can't really talk to me about school or what you're learning, and I can't talk to you about what matters to me. I don't think you've ever asked me about what I'm interested in."

"I can change," Alan said earnestly. "What does interest you?"

I almost laughed, but I kept my face serious, as I said, "No, I'm sure we'd be better off not seeing each other."

"I've goofed again," Alan said, shaking his head.

"And you have to stop that, too," I said. "Nobody wants to hear people whine about what they're doing wrong, and about what everybody else is doing wrong. I think you ought to look for a girl who's studying physics, the way you are."

"There aren't many. I don't meet girls much in my classes."

"There must be some."

"But they're not pretty."

I looked at him, with his pale face and squinty eyes, and wondered if he'd ever find a girl who would put up with him. All he seemed to want was a pretty face and a girl who listened to him. There must be some boys out there who wanted more.

"So let's say good-bye. And I should tell you something before we separate. Maybe it will make it easier for you."

"What?"

"I like Ginger Rogers and Fred Astaire."

CHAPTER 23

July 1948
Bronx–Brooklyn

R ose had suggested double-dating again. She said Jerry had another friend, not as smart as Alan, but nice-looking and a good dancer.

"No," I said, almost reluctantly. Not that I wasn't interested in boys. Some of the pilots who passed through the floors of Air France made me hungry for romance. A few of them smiled at me—at most of the young girls who worked there—and one of them even stopped to talk to me when he came by.

"How are you getting on, Nicole?"

"Oh, just fine, and you, Charles?"

"My head's in the clouds most of the time." Both of us laughed. "Is Dupuis giving you a hard time?"

"No, not at all. He's really very kind to me."

"Hmm! Maybe you'd better be careful. He's probably got his eye on you."

When I told Rose about him, she said, "Well, you should have given him a little encouragement."

"How do I do that?"

"Like when he said that M. Dupuis had his eye on you, you could have said something like, 'Oh, I don't think anybody has an eye on me,' or you could have said—maybe smiling right at him—'I wish somebody younger did.'"

Rose was my mentor. She knew how to meet boys, how to behave with them, how to encourage them, and how to get rid of them and move on when she had lost interest. She was very pleased that I had stopped seeing Alan.

"He was hopeless," she said. "I told you so."

"Yes, but Rose, you went out with him longer than I did."

"A big mistake," she said. "I guess I thought I could change him, but Nicole, remember, you can never change a boy. Take it from me."

FOR THE TIME BEING, I put my interest in boys aside. Simone enjoyed her job as a receptionist. She and the hygienist had worked out an armistice, and she liked meeting the patients and looking through all the magazines in the dentist's office when nobody was around.

She was also ready to move. Every weekend in June, either she or I, and often both of us together, followed up on the rent ads in the newspaper. There weren't very many of them. Most apartments were too expensive, even with my salary and hers.

"You're supposed to use only a quarter of your money on rent," she told me. "I read it in the paper. So with your forty dollars and my twenty-five, that makes sixty-five dollars a week, and one quarter of that is . . . is . . ."

I dropped the paper and said, "We'll never find a place."

But we looked anyway. One was sharing an apartment with a cranky old lady who asked for eighty dollars and said we couldn't use the kitchen. Another one in the east Bronx had two tiny rooms with a small refrigerator in one of the rooms, and no sink, except in the bathroom. The place needed painting, and it rented for seventy-five dollars.

"We'll never find a place," Simone said, discouraged.

But we did. Dr. Lyons's sister had a friend who lived in Flatbush, Brooklyn, in her own house, and had re-modeled her basement. She was a war widow and was looking for one or two reliable girls who came with good references.

We traveled out to Flatbush on the subway. Neither of us had ever been to Brooklyn before, and we were uncertain about what to expect. We found the house on a street with high, leafy trees lining the sidewalks. Those trees made me suddenly very happy.

For close to a year now, I had lived up in the Bronx on Grand Concourse, with few trees and lots of cars. It made me realize how much I had missed any kind of greenery. My town of Aix-les-Bains had trees and flowers everywhere, and close by, the hills and the country.

The house even had a little green lawn in front of it, with a row of purple irises standing stiffly at attention along its borders.

A young woman with a sad face opened the door. "Are you Simone?" she asked me.

"No, *Madame,* this is Simone. I'm Nicole."

"Well, come in, girls, come in. My friend's brother recommended you highly, Simone. He said you were very pleasant and very reliable."

Simone tried to look pleasant and reliable, and so did I. The apartment seemed very quiet as she led us through it. There was a piano with a framed picture of an American soldier on top of it, which we tried to avoid looking at.

"There is a door on the side of the house," she told us, "so you'd have your own private entrance. You wouldn't have to come through my house as you're doing now."

We followed her down the stairs as she led us to the door on the side. When she opened it to show us the apartment, I gasped out loud.

"I know it's only one room," she said apologetically, "but it's pretty large. My husband and I bought the house before he was sent overseas in 1944. He thought . . . well, we both thought . . . the war was coming to an end, and he wanted to finish the basement and rent it out to help pay for the mortgage. I've just gotten around to it because . . . I haven't been able to handle it before. I'm working now. I teach music, but I do need to supplement my income to pay off the mortgage."

The apartment was one very large room, with a kitchenette and a separate bathroom. But what had made me gasp was that through the two large windows at the back, we could see a garden—a real garden with a lawn and beds of flowers.

"You would be able to use the garden, of course. My husband used to do all the gardening himself," she said in a shaky voice, "but now, I have a gardener who comes every two months and keeps the lawn mowed and weeds the flowers. In between, I try to take care of it, but I guess I don't always have the time."

"*Madame*," I said, "perhaps we could do the gardening. It would be such a pleasure to work in a garden. And Simone would enjoy it, too. Isn't that right, Simone?"

Simone didn't appear as eager, but she nodded and smiled.

"Well, why don't we wait and see," said the woman, whose name was Mrs. Walker. "I've had the gardener for a few years now, and he's very reliable. But if you wanted to help in between by watering and weeding, it would help me quite a bit. Maybe I could even take, say, five dollars off the rent."

"What is the rent?" Simone asked, and the two of us waited nervously for her answer.

"Well, I was thinking of about seventy-five dollars. We're very well located. Transportation is good, and so is shopping. And the neighborhood is safe, even at night."

Simone and I looked at each other. Seventy-five dollars was ten dollars more than we could afford.

Mrs. Walker continued, "Of course, if you do the gardening, I would take five dollars off, and the rent would be seventy dollars a month, and that includes gas and electricity. Don't you want to check the stove and refrigerator? They're practically new. I bought them from a neighbor who moved out to Long Island."

I suppose the stove and refrigerator were fine, and I think the plumbing in the bathroom was also fine. Mrs. Walker pointed out that the walls had been freshly painted, but all I really saw was the garden. Even through the windows, I could already smell the grass.

CHAPTER 24

August 1948
Flatbush, Brooklyn

Cousin Harriet exploded when I told her I intended to move.

"Why?" she demanded. "After all we've done for you, why would you want to move?"

"I appreciate all you've done, Cousin Harriet—and Cousin Jake, too—but I realize it's too crowded with me living here. I'm sure Evvie would like to have her own room back again."

Evvie shook her head. "No," she said. "I'm sorry you're going."

"You'll come and visit," I said to her. "Maybe the three of us—you, Simone, and I—can go places together."

"If you really mean it," she said shyly.

But Harriet continued arguing. "And I really don't know if it looks respectable for two young girls to live all by themselves."

"Simone is nineteen and I'm eighteen now. Both of us have jobs, and we won't have any trouble paying the rent."

"Well, French people must be different. Here, a girl lives with her family until she marries. And besides, you're only giving me a couple of weeks' notice. You're supposed to give us a month. I think you should pay a month's rent."

"Ma!" Evvie said. "Don't make a fuss. She's old enough to know what she wants."

COUSIN JAKE SAID it was fine. I didn't have to pay anything extra. He asked how we planned to move our furniture.

"Right now, we don't have much furniture, but Rose's father has a truck, and he's offered to help. He'll pick me up first, with my clothes, and then Simone. Her parents are giving her a card table, one chair, a little rug, and her bed."

"I could give you a few things, too," Jake said quietly, when Harriet wasn't around. "There's a sofa in our reception room we're planning to replace. It's a little worn but still comfortable. I could also let you have two or three folding chairs if your friend's father doesn't mind picking them up."

We moved at the beginning of August. I had two weeks' vacation, and Simone had only one. The hygienist gave us a droopy rubber plant that needed more light than it was getting in the office, and a painting Dr. Lyons felt inappropriate for his office. It was a still life of a table that displayed a large chocolate cake and a bowl of sugared doughnuts.

We needed a chest of drawers, and our landlady offered us one. She helped carry it downstairs. It was a handsome oak chest, hardly used, and we both realized it must have belonged to her late husband.

Mrs. Walker's first name was Grace, and she insisted we call her that. The first night we moved in, she brought us a pot of chili and a salad.

"Please join us," we asked.

"Oh, no," she said, looking at the mess of boxes, furniture, and clothes. "I'm sure you have plenty to do."

We insisted and, finally, she agreed. The only problem was that we still had no dishes. Grace went back upstairs and brought back dishes she said we could keep, and some forks, knives, and spoons she said she and her husband had used on camping trips.

She was our first guest at the apartment, even if she had brought the food, the dishes, and the silverware. The garden faced southwest, and the sunlight streamed through the windows as we ate. Grace tried not to speak about her husband, but she couldn't help herself. They had been married only two years, and they had so many plans that would never be realized. He was killed in 1945, shortly before the war ended.

As she spoke, I saw in her face the kind of suffering I had believed unknown to Americans.

"Let me know if I can help you in any way," she offered as she left.

And then, there was just Simone and I, sitting there all alone.

"Are you frightened?" she asked, looking around at the big mess.

"A little," I admitted.

"What should we do first?"

"I guess we should hang up the clothes."

"Did you bring hangers?"

"No, I never thought of it."

Both of us looked at the sofa. It was a faded green.

"We could make slipcovers," I said. "Do you know how to sew?"

"No, do you?"

"No, but maybe we could just throw a piece of pretty fabric over it."

"Do you have a piece of pretty fabric?"

By this time I was laughing, and soon Simone was laughing, too. We realized that we didn't have many important items. But nothing would be impossible for us now. We would learn as we went along.

We spent the rest of the evening moving the furniture around. The chest, we pushed to one side of the room, along with the bed. We placed the sofa, which would also serve as my bed until we could afford a bed for me, on the wall facing the garden, with the little rug in front of it. We folded our underwear, stockings, and shirts, and put them into the chest. Our dresses and coats, we piled inside the two closets. The painting we stood on one side of the couch until we bought the hardware to put it up on the wall, and the droopy plant on the other. The card table wobbled, but we placed it near the stove and refrigerator and grouped our four mismatched chairs around it.

By the end of the evening, we looked around proudly at our own apartment. Within a few days, we would be able to buy whatever we needed for day-to-day living.

"Tomorrow, we have to buy hangers, blankets, towels, toilet paper, and soap."

"We'll also need hooks and wires to hang that picture," Simone added.

"Do you like it?"

"Not particularly, but we don't have anything else."

"Let's put it in the bathroom. And, you know, I can get some posters from Air France. Some of them are very pretty. One of them shows the Eiffel Tower, and another one, the Jardin des Tuilleries. Maybe we can use them until we find something better."

"Maybe we could get a poster from the Museum of Modern Art. They have beautiful posters, and they don't cost too much."

"Maybe we could . . ."

There was no end of maybes.

But right now, the sun was setting over the garden. We sat on the sofa and watched the sky turn from blue to pink to black.

It wasn't easy getting ready for bed, since we had forgotten about towels and sheets. Grace had thoughtfully put a roll of toilet paper in the bathroom and a bathmat near the shower. But ingenuity goes a long way, and soon, the two of us settled ourselves in for the night. Simone slept on her bed, and I on the sofa. It was a warm night, and at first, we didn't need blankets. But later, as it cooled down, I woke up feeling chilly. I piled a few of my sweaters and shirts on top of me and tried to get back to sleep.

I could hear Simone's breath, easy and steady, from her bed. I remembered my sister, and the sound of her breathing when she shared a room with me on the Avenue du Petit Port. The charm bracelet lay under my pillow. I reached for it and held it in my hand.

It made me think about my family, and about the new life that was beginning for me without them. I had their photographs, and as I lay there in the dark, I thought, now I can hang some of them up on one wall. And maybe Simone could use another wall for pictures of people she cared about.

My father had once said, "Remember, Nicole, there is nothing in this world you cannot do."

He was mistaken. I could not bring them back, but I could try to live my life in a way he and my mother would approve.

I rose and moved over to the window. There was no moonlight, and the garden outside lay dark and mysterious. But in the morning, I knew I would wake up to green grass and bright flowers. I could feel the little charms on Jacqueline's bracelet in my hand. It was part of my past, but it would always be with me, along with all the memories of my family.

I stood by the window while Simone slept soundly, and suddenly I felt grateful. After being lost in America for nearly a year, I could finally think of it as home.

ABOUT THIS BOOK

The story of Nicole Nieman is based on the life of Fanny Krieger, a close friend who lives only a few blocks away from me in San Francisco.

Both of us became friends more than thirty years ago, because of two bad boys—her son and mine. When they

Fanny Bienstock Krieger, age seventeen.

attended elementary school, we spent a good deal of time in the principal's office, and nobody ever quite determined which boy was worse. (Both of them, to our surprise and delight, grew up to be decent human beings, good husbands and fathers.)

I noticed at that time that Fanny spoke with an unusual accent, and when I asked, she told me that she had been born in France, and came to the United States when she was seventeen, in 1947. Her parents and little sister had been taken by the Nazis during the war, and all of them were killed in Poland at the Auschwitz concentration camp.

For me, as a teenager here in America, the war had been almost fun. I was in high school and helped in the war effort by selling U.S. government bonds, knitting scarves for soldiers, growing "victory gardens" of fruits and vegetables, and writing letters to soldiers. We suffered no hunger, no cold, and no fear. Nobody I knew well was in the service. I lied about my age and said I was eighteen when I was really sixteen so that I could dress up and dance with soldiers at the various canteens around New York City, where I then lived.

All that time, Fanny, a year younger than I, was hiding from the Gestapo. She suffered hunger, cold, and always the fear of being found out and taken away by the Nazis because she was Jewish.

About thirty years ago, I decided to write her story, which I did in a novel called *A Pocket Full of Seeds*. But some stories don't finish. And this was one of them. "The worst and best year of my life," she said at that time, "was my first year in America." So this is a fictionalized story about that year.

There is much more that happened later on. Fanny left New York and ended up in Houston, working for the Belgian consulate. She married, had a daughter and a son, and now has four grandchildren. Despite some early setbacks, she eventually became a successful businesswoman. Today, she lives in San Francisco and has become a famous figure in the fly-fishing world. She travels a good deal and enjoys a colorful and exciting life.

Rose, her friend in the story, continues to be her friend in real life. She lives in Houston and is a retired French teacher. She has two children and three grandchildren. She and Fanny visit each other as often as they can.

Simone (her real name is Margot) ended up marrying the man she dreamily talks of in the book. They live in Switzerland and enjoy their children and grandchildren. Fanny continues to see her here and in Europe.

Françoise (really Claudine), Nicole's friend who gave Jacqueline the charm bracelet, now lives in Paris. She and Fanny remain good friends.

Fanny is not a friend anyone wants to lose. Of all the people I know, she is the most generous and most willing to help anyone in need. When our school district decided to integrate its schools, Fanny was one of the most ardent supporters. The two of us, over the years, have spoken in schools around the Bay Area, discussing her story and the horrors of war.

Fanny is a great cook, and her dinner parties are famous. She is also one of the most ingenious people I know. As her daughter, Sharon, remembers, one of Fanny's favorite sayings is, "If you can't get through the front door, try the back door."

On a lighter note, I must add that Fanny continues to love banana splits, but she no longer eats one every day.

—M.S.